The Dolocher

European P. Douglas

Also by European P. Douglas

The Brave Festival

The Great Brutality

The Case for Skeletons

Michelin

The Story of Furniture Anderson

Copyright © 2014 European P. Douglas
All rights reserved.
ISBN: 1494372819
ISBN-13: 978-1494372811

Chapter 1

It was only apt that the hardest rain fell from the blackest clouds when that monster Thomas Olocher was brought to 'The Black Dog' prison. He had killed three women in the most gruesome fashion and his trial had been the talk of the city for weeks now. He had finally been found guilty and sentenced to hang. Why he had been sent to 'The Black Dog,' or Newgate to give it its proper title, was less clear as this was a well-known debtors prison and further from the hanging place than was normally the case.

The Magistrate had sentenced him to death but made no mention of where he was to be kept until the execution. This decision had been made by someone else but by whom there were no answers to be found. The rumour mill spread word of an escape bid, that rich and powerful friends of Olocher; the Pinking Dindies for example, would be better able to free him from a relatively under guarded debtors prison than from one of the proper gaols in the city.

For the journey from the courthouse to the gaol Olocher was sat shackled at wrist and ankle flanked by two big soldiers and with two more sitting on the opposite bench facing him, with two more standing on platforms at the back of the cart. Their attitude was that of men used to transporting all kinds of vermin to prison; their eyes not making contact with their cargo, their shoulders set back and straight, ready at a moment's notice to strike out if need be. To be truthful they had the look of men who no more wanted to be in Ireland than the devils bed; they didn't need a reason to strike out.

Olocher himself looked a little worse for wear; his eyes wore the puffy padding of a recent beating, which made it look as though he was arrogantly squinting at the world as he passed by, a face that many a woman feared ever seeing and one that was made all the more grotesque with the blemishes, swelling and cuts that adorned it now. The escorting soldiers must have had a good go at him every evening after his court appearances- no more than he deserved.

Olocher's crimes were vicious and frenzied; he had slashed the throats of his victims but not before he had savaged their bodies with his blades. It is said that he would knock his victim to the ground and then pounce on her using his weight to hold her down. He would then flail wildly with a long stiff and sharp knife in each hand, slashing into her (and often slicing his own legs in the process- a fact that brought about the most astonishment in court when he was asked to display his scarred and knotted thighs to the magistrate) It was said that he would listen to their pitiful crying and watch as they tried to slither away from him and that he would wait deathly silent and let them think they had escaped before grabbing them by the head and whispering something awful to them before slashing their throats. What he actually said to them was a matter of salacious gossip as the only witness to any of his crimes was a young girl of fourteen called Mary Sommers who hadn't heard what Olocher had said as he killed her aunt while Mary hid in a closet, clutching her breath in her throat and trying not to scream out. Olocher never even knew she was there.

When asked in court what he had said to the women he answered simply,

"It wasn't me who killed them, so I never said anything to those women." Witnesses put him at the scenes of all the crimes and there were no shortage of women who had been on his bad side over the last few years. One in particular had nearly been killed when he pounced on her and pounded at her with his fists much in the manner of the later killings; he hadn't gone that far that time but the woman remembered that he had hit himself on the knee so hard during the attack that he limped away afterwards. A former workmate from Olocher's time on the boats told of his having torn holes in his trouser pockets where he could gain quick access to knives strapped to either of his thighs and how he had seen him fight one time on the docks in Liverpool and swing wildly with knives in both hands. More than a couple of tavern keepers could tell of his temper and his threats about using those very blades. When presented with all of this and pressed again about what he said to the women before he killed them he once again answered that it wasn't him so he couldn't have said anything to them.

To most people there was no doubt that he would have received the death penalty even if he had not irked the Magistrate by continuing to deny culpability but there were still some who thought he could have gotten off lighter with just a confession. When the Magistrate passed sentence it is said that Olocher's face turned a shade darker and he could be seen reaching for his thighs as though he would take out those blades there and then in the courthouse and launch himself at the Magistrate in that frenzy so vividly described by Mary Sommers.

As the blacksmith Timothy Mullins watched the cart approach the gates of the prison he couldn't help notice that the pigs that seemed to fill the streets these last few months didn't have to be prodded and kicked out of the way, they stepped aside as though the carriage was carrying royalty. It was so noticeable that he was not the only one to see it and a man cried out in jest as he pointed to the splitting sea of porcine subjects,

"All hail the King of the Swine!" to which there was much laughter and jeering of those who were huddled under the shop awnings to avoid this latest burst of foul weather. Mullins looked at Olocher who seemed not to notice the insult or any of the cacophony it created. It was possible that there was swelling in his ears as well Mullins supposed on seeing the wounded face that reminded him of his own deformity.

Mullins had heard tales of what Olocher had done but the man in front of him now did not fit with the image he'd formed in his head of what type of barbarian would do something like this. It was clear from his bearing that Olocher was from higher stock. He was known to always have money and was always buying rounds in pubs he frequented- Mullins had never been on the receiving end of this generosity but he had heard of it. It was said that Olocher was of noble blood but though he still had his money he worked rough jobs and spent time in taverns to escape the tedium of civilised life. There were rumours that when he was not around that Olocher tidied himself up and lived as a member of the upper classes from where he was from for a period under his real name (which no one ever seemed to know) before sliding back to the unshaven and cravenly debauched Thomas Olocher. Of course Dublin in 1786 was a place that had no shortage of rumour and in many cases it was the rumour or the legend that held sway over the people minds in the place of truth and facts.

It was filthily black now and dull water sloshed down the sides of the street, sloshing mud and animal waste across the uneven and cracking cobblestones and filling the sewer that ran along the side of the prison with new power and energy. There was a smell rising from it that mingled with the wet people huddled together and the smell of the crackling fires inside the buildings around, the result being a putrid amalgamation of everyday life covered in faeces and doused in urine.

The gates of the goal cracked and rattled from within and then there was a loud creak and scraping noise as it opened and ran across the uneven stones beneath it, the wood splintered and cracked from everyday use and poor maintenance. The gaoler and two guards came out and spoke to one of the soldiers who handed the gaoler some papers with the seal of the court on them. Mullins could see the unease on the face of the gaoler and he picked up a couple of words on the wind as he remonstrated with the soldier, 'here?' 'not suitable' and 'dangerous' were the ones he could make out but the tinny voice and the shape of his mouth as he spoke gave away all the fears of the gaoler. This was no place for a murderer like Olocher he must be saying and Mullins was in full agreement with that. The soldier had a look of boredom and he pressed the papers to the gaoler's chest and then pointed up to the top of one of the towers of the prison.

"Yeah" shouted someone from the crowd, which seemed to have grown steadily since Mullins last looked, "keep him in the tower and hang him from up there!" There were murmurs of agreement.

"No, stick him in the 'Nunnery'" another called out and the crowd swelled with laughter again.

The soldier turned gruffly to the crowd,

"You lot go back about your business!" he shouted at the crowd. No one moved but the soldier was already facing back to the cart and telling the others to take Olocher into the gaol.

The springs creaked and the wood of the cart moaned as the first soldiers got out and stood to one side. Olocher was made to stand then and two more of the soldiers pushed him off and into the clutches of the first two soldiers before they too jumped down from the cart.

"These men will be added to your guards for the time being. I suggest that you increase security yourself while he is here" Mullins heard the lead soldier say and he cocked his head at Olocher. The gaoler nodded resignedly and pointed inside the gates to where the soldiers ushered Olocher. The gaoler gave one more rueful look at the people gathered outside before he went inside and pulled that gate behind him. The remaining soldier got back into the cart and it cantered off down the street back in the direction it came from. The filth splashing as it did.

The rain began to subside and the crowd began to disperse. Mullins pulled his hood up over his thick black hair so that only his face with its almost black eyes and his scarred cheek and wide nose were visible in the darkening light.

"There'll be no one sleeping in there tonight" a voice said beside him and Mullins turned and saw Cleaves, his friend from the whisky house on Cook Street not fifty feet from where they stood now.

"I doubt it" he answered.

"Are you going to the tavern?" Cleaves asked looking in its direction.

"No, I'm going home" Cleaves nodded, his hunched frame lost in a thick coat two or three sizes too big for him. He looked small and decrepit because of his bent over stance but his shoulders were wide and his hands large. Cleaves had eyes that were such a pale blue that they elucidated sympathy for him even when he sought none. People had to meet him many times before they were able to make out the creased face and his large bulbous ears and bent nose. He was not ugly as sin but getting there but his eyes were hypnotic even to a tough blacksmith like Timothy Mullins.

At this moment those eyes were trained on the high tower of the gaol and Mullins followed their gaze and they could see a candle was burning at the top room.

"That must be where they are putting him" Cleaves said.

"He'll be hard pressed to escape from up there without killing himself" Cleaves nodded in agreement. "I bet there's a few in there tonight who wished they had paid their debts now eh Tim?" Cleaves grinned nudging his bony elbow into Mullins' ribs.

"You can be sure of that Cleaves" he answered.

Just then there was a noise coming from within the gaol walls. There was shouting, female shouting echoing from the basement of the goal. A male voice rose against them but the shrill noises continued and slaps of hand against faces could be heard and women screaming filtered out into the street.

"That'll be the girls in the 'Nunnery' complaining about him being under the same roof" Cleaves said without humour this time.

"Who could blame them" Mullins said and he patted Cleaves on the shoulder as he began to walk away and make his way home.

Chapter 2

There were ten women in the 'Nunnery' on the day that Thomas Olocher was sentenced to hang, though they had no idea that he was going to be housed amongst them until the cart carrying him pulled up outside in the rain. The 'Nunnery' was in the basement of 'The Black Dog' and there were windows at ground level with the street where the women could see outside. At the best of times they still had to stand well clear of the barred slots however as running sewers along the side of the road would seep in through the natural drain the windows provided leaving the air in the basement dungeon as putrid as any tavern toilet- it actually took a few days to rid the ammonia uric smell once the women were granted their freedom. Today, with its terrible downpours there was a stream of filth threshing through and most of the floor inside the 'Nunnery' was slick with all kinds of street and human waste.

Kate O'Leary, who went by Kitty to some, was huddled amongst the other women at the corner furthest from the windows on hay they had piled to stop it from getting wet. They had a sodden barrier of clothes that held back the dank liquids from getting to the edge of the hay. Kate was very small and was quite warm between the heavier bodies of the other women around her. Her mousy brown hair was unwashed and greasy and her pale face looked tired and drawn- her cheekbones very prominent due to the shrunken eye sockets. It was clear that she was a pretty girl but it was hard to see at this moment in time. Her deep blue eyes had a terrible sorrow in them as she looked about at her current predicament.

This was her first time in 'The Black Dog' and she was not here for the owning of debts. The self-righteous Parish Watch had grabbed her from the clutches of a customer in a lane off Fishamble Street a few nights previous and had presented her at the gates for incarceration. As you have probably guessed the 'Nunnery' was a local name for the basement dungeon where prostitutes were thrown from time to time. They were never arrested but instead were rounded up by puritan or displeased Parish Watchmen who had no trouble putting food in their bellies or a place to sleep under their bodies. They were hypocrites into the bargain as Kate recognised one of the men who brought her here as a customer from a few weeks previous.

The women would be housed in the cell for a few days generally with no formal charge brought against them and then they would be cast out as more were shipped in or when someone paid for them to get out (which didn't happen very often.) It was often said that things were much easier back in Gaoler Hawkins day when a quick handy or suck would have you back on the streets that same evening.

This current gaoler, James Brick (known by the ladies as jimmy the Prick) was a different breed of animal though and he was not swayed by such carnal bribes. He made sure that the women who came under his charge did not enjoy their time at this establishment. It was he who had decided that the women could spend their time in the sewer running dungeon; they were scum after all as he reasoned and the rest of his clientele were just good fellows a little down on their luck and owing a few bob here and there. Brick had put fear into the women earlier in the year by saying that they should be careful about accepting the offers of men to pay for them to get out as Thomas Olocher himself had paid for a girl to get out and they all knew how she had ended up.

Kate drew some measure of satisfaction once she realised why his face was so ashen that morning, there was a sense of poetic justice that he was going to have to have Olocher himself under his guard. The fear in his face was scrawled as plainly as any picture pamphlet. It was no joy for the women to have to share a building with this hater of their species and Kate was glad that they had all to huddle in this corner to escape the sewer water and she could nestle safely in the mass of women.

They heard the cart arrive and the gates opening, there was some chat and then somebody shouted something and there was laughter but still they were not sure what was happening. It was only after the gates were closed that they knew that someone was being escorted to one of the tower cells; someone in shackles as they could hear the jingling metal and the halted steps and the chains pinging off the smooth stone steps of the stairs.

One of the women asked their own guard at the door who was being brought up to the good rooms. The guard turned and looked with pity at the women and it was this look of pity that terrified the girls and made them aware before he answered who it was that was being ferried up the stairs. There was immediate uproar.

"He can't be here in the same place that women are!"

"Oh Mother of Christ we'll all be killed!"

"You have to let us out of here! You have to!"

"Ladies, I'd advise you to be quiet or there will be trouble" the guard said in a harsh whisper.

"There's already trouble- Olocher is here!"

"Be quiet before the gaoler comes back down for your own sakes women" he said to them.

There was no let-up in the pleading and cursing and the gaoler did indeed come down after a time. He went into the cell and the women drew back from him as he slapped at them to be quiet.

"What's all the fuckin' racket in here?" he asked looking about wildly at them. Kate was afraid to say anything now but some of the other women didn't hold back.

"We have to be let out, we can't be under the same roof as him" one of them said.

"You're safe down here" the gaoler said "and you won't be going anywhere, you lot are no better than him anyway" At this the women protested loudly. Kate as well as she did not appreciate at all being lumped in with a twisted killer such as Olocher. The gaoler didn't say anything back to them he just started to lash out. He slapped those closest to him across the face and kicked them over in the slime on the floor before turning and leaving the cell with its crying and trembling inhabitants.

"Don't feed them tonight!" he said to the guard as he walked out.

Chapter 3

That night Kate had managed to fall asleep despite the protestations of her belly and the stench of her surroundings. The guard at their door had taken some small pity on them and had put some blankets through the bars to cover the women while they huddled together on the damp hay to sleep and a stale hard lump of bread was tossed in between them. She knew that she dreamed every night but they were never of any real substance, just images mixed up and rearranged of things that happened before in her life or exaggerations of imagings she might have upon seeing something odd or startling.

On this night she thought she was dreaming for a long time before she realised she was awake. Once she did she sat up in fright, listening. Her jostling woke some of the other women.

"Go back to sleep darlin'" one of them said as though to a child.

"Listen" Kate said sitting up straighter still.

"What is it Kitty?" The women who were still asleep started to stir as the noise Kate spoke of began to register in their consciousness's. There was a low howling that at first could have been mistaken for the wind but when they listened they knew it wasn't. It was a woman screaming though at a very low volume and then it began to grow louder. All of the women were awake now and they took stock to see if any of their number was missing but they were all still there. They could hear the guards moving around a little and then the screaming grew even louder until there was no denying what it was anymore. It was a woman screaming and the sound was coming from somewhere up in the tower.

"Olocher is killing someone up there!" the women shouted at the guards.

"Be quiet in there!" one of them snapped back but his attention was on the stairs to where he could hear the other guards calling out to one another and asking what was going on. His face was scared and white in the darkness.

"Olocher's asleep in his bed" someone called down but the screaming was still going and getting louder.

And then a new noise began, not unlike the first but from outside this time and the women looked through the bars and they could see that there were many pigs, more than would be usual in the same place and they were whining lowly in the same way as the screaming from upstairs.

"It's the banshee" one of the women said and no one knew any better to correct her. They clutched closer together in natural defensiveness. Outside the porcine chorus grew in intensity and the guards looked out to the see what was happening. The squeals grew frenzied from the wild animals and an agitation began to run through them as though they were in pain. The squealing grew to such a pitch that it was painful to listen to and all the women and the guards had to cover their ears.

"What the fuck is going on here?" James Brick asked bursting into the courtyard just above the steps to the dungeon. He was pulling on a coat over his bed clothes.

"We don't know" was the inept reply from one of the guards.

"What is this noise?" Brick shouted above the din.

"Pigs outside the gate"

"Pigs?" Brick was clearly confused but also a little relieved.

"There's another noise coming from up there but the guards up there say Olocher is asleep in his bed and they don't know where the noise in coming from"

Just then there was a terrific thump at the wooden gates of the prison.

"Now what?" Brick said exasperated, the apprehension back in his face.

"Someone's trying to get in!" a guard called out.

"Where are the soldiers?" Brick called out. There was another massive thump against the gates and they creaked with the force.

"Keep your hair on in there" a voice called from without the gates "It's these bleedin' pigs bashing against the gate!" It was one of the soldiers who was guarding from outside. They could hear him trying to shoo the animals and they heard the heavy wet slap of the soldier's baton on the back flesh of the pigs. "There's a fuckin' tonne of them out here" he went on. The squealing was reaching a point where nothing else could be heard. More thumping came against the gates but it was almost silent at that point, a visual throbbing of wood pulse in the lantern fire sparkled shadowplay.

The noise was unbearable now and though men were talking, shouting, no voice could be heard save that of the screaming pigs and the original scream of no fixed origin. Everyone had their ears covered and no one knew what to do so all stood rooted to where they were. Kate could feel the trembling of the women about her as some cried and others shook as if to try to rid themselves of the sounds in their head or to try wake themselves from what was clearly, to them at least, a terrible nightmare.

And then all the noises stopped and there was silence. For ten seconds still more not a soul moved. Kate looked out the window and she could see the army of pigs disperse down different streets, some stopping and sniffing at the kerbsides for food and otherwise acting as the normal nuisance that they were.

"Check on Olocher" the soldier from outside shouted in but it was said with no immediacy.

"Do it" Brick said and the women's guard left his post and ran up the stairs. Kate listened to his feet slapping on the stone steps and then heard the rattle of keys and his voice from the distance,

"Get up there now" and then she heard the heavy clanking of the lock and the door of the cell opening. Then there was silence for a moment.

Kate had a terrible feeling in her body at this silence. She was imagining the guard going to the bed where Thomas Olocher was sleeping and drawing back the blanket find it stuffed with hay and no sign of Olocher. She imagined him loose in the goal and somehow being in this very room right now waiting to kill them as they slept. She could almost hear his echoed breathing against the cold stone walls. Involuntarily she darted glances around the room and though there was none big enough to hide a man of any size every black space multiplied the terror in her soul.

"He's escaped" she heard herself say. The others looked at her in horror and it was clear to her that they had all had the same idea though none was happy that it had been spoken aloud.

There was a commotion of running and talking from those up in the tower and the women's fears seemed to be correct. They huddled closer together and waited grimly for the news that he had escaped.

"You better come here sir" one of the guards called down.

"Why what's going on?" Brick asked (he was known not to like walking up those stairs if he could avoid it.)

"You better come see" the voice came back down and there was leaning in tone towards something dreadful.

"Oh for fuck sake" Brick said as he began to ascend the stairs.

"Wait!" one of the women called out, "we have no guard" Brick looked In at the women.

"You'll be fine for a few minutes" he said sarcastically and he continued on up. The women listened again for that dreaded word 'escaped.' The gaoler seemed to take an age shuffling up those stairs and there was no longer any commotion or noise anywhere else.

When he finally got to the top they could hear some speaking and then the gaoler crying out,

"What? How?" and this to the women confirmed their horrid beliefs.

"Oh god what are we going to do?" one of them wailed.

"It's ok Betty" Kate said rubbing her arm, "Don't forget we're still locked in here, and it's as hard to get in as it is to get out"

"Shhh, I can't hear what's going on?" the woman closest to the cell door said. They all listened again and they could hear what seemed to be the voice of Brick muttering about something but no one else was speaking. In a few moments they heard the heavy uniforms of the soldiers as they came down the stairs. When the soldiers got to the bottom of the stairs they stood at the gate and opened the hatch and one of them said something to the soldier outside.

"What's going on?" Betty called out to them. One of the soldiers looked in to the cell and surveyed the women, probably trying to see if he been a customer of any of them.

"You don't have to worry your pretty little heads darlin's" he said

"Why is that?" Betty asked.

"Our old pal Olocher is dead"

"Dead?" Kate asked, though there were no questions from the rest as they were just relieved to be out of mortal danger.

"Killed himself with a blade he must have smuggled in" the soldier said and he left them and went back to the other soldier in the yard.

The women knew at this point that there was going to be no sleep tonight. An officer from the army was first to arrive, followed closely by an army doctor and then some men who looked like they might be involved in the legal profession. There was comings and goings all night and the gaoler was obviously under severe pressure as to why this had been able to happen.

"Was he not searched when he got here?" the officer asked incredulous.

"He came straight from the courthouse under armed guard, I was sure he would have been searched already" Brick replied.

"What type of a prison are you running here you idiot!" the officer shouted. Brick was displeased in the extreme but he was too clever to answer back and make things worse for himself. Kate however had no shame about enjoying his squirming and embarrassment.

The same questions were asked throughout the night and in all the furore about Olocher's death it was almost possible to forget about the wailing and the screeching of the pigs outside. Kate wondered if it had indeed been the banshee they heard- the ancient foreteller of death and then she wondered about the three knocks that also signalled death, had that been how many times the pigs had barraged against the gates? She couldn't be sure but she thought so.

"That was the oddest thing with the pigs wasn't it?" she said to the others.

"I've never heard of, or seen anything like it in me life!" Betty replied.

"What was it all about?" another of the women asked but none among them had even a guess to make. It was baffling beyond description, especially since there were so many pigs about the streets in general and everyone was used to their habits by now.

Chapter 4

There must have been at least two hundred people at Gallows Green at the scaffold where Thomas Olocher was to be hanged the following morning. It had been arranged solely for his execution and there was none other scheduled for the drop that morning which was an unusual practice. The weather was fine though chilly with a strong low sun that blinded those who caught its glare or that reflected off any metal or glass surface. It had been raining overnight again and the wet and filth covered cobbles threw the glare further still like an expanding golden river in the street.

As is always the way there was much hubbub in the crowd though in secret it was a nervous excitement that thrilled through each private individual; the lust for death by justice loses a lot of its sheen and romanticism when faced with the actual hanging itself- the rickety scaffold, the thick rope, the hooded killer and the priest, those who must oversee the hanging. It was truly morbidly sickening but even those who were veterans of this queasiness could not bring themselves to stay away from such a momentous meeting out of justice as that for Thomas Olocher.

It was only ten in the morning but there was a whiskey cabin atmosphere spreading throughout the crowd, a kind of drunkenness that fed on the fears and trepidations of the people who had gathered there. The noise of voices continued to rise and rise and was punctured here and there by the cacophony of street sellers trying to hawk anything imaginable and the shouts of those who shooed beggars or pickpockets who were always present for large gatherings.

As the time for the spectacle grew closer the crowd grew larger and at the appointed hour there was close to five hundred packed into the space around the streets surrounding the gallows. Mullins had arrived late and made his way through the crowds until he found some faces that he knew, Cleaves among them. They nodded to him but continued with their conversation. Mullins looked around at the crowd until he heard something that piqued his interest.

"What's this about pigs?" he asked the men.

"There was hundreds of pigs screaming and stomping the gates of the prison last night!" one of them said.

"It wasn't hundreds!" Cleaves contradicted him.

"I heard something unnatural last night alright" Mullins said, "but I had no clue what it was"

"Well now you know but it's still a mystery as to what they were up to" Cleaves said.

"Maybe the Pinking Dindies sent them to try to break old Olocher out" Mullins joked and the men all laughed.

"Jokes aside though, there are still rumours that they may try to spring him from here today" Cleaves said

"I see a few men over by the weavers there that fit the bill perfectly" Mullins said and they all looked over to where he nodded.

There were ten men who conversed in a close circle, all very well dressed and carrying swords as part of this attire. They were all very well groomed as well and were taller than average and though not fat in the slightest they had the healthy bulk of the well fed upper classes. It was of course possible that there were some of the gang known as the Pinking Dindies but few amongst the lower classes knew any of these people by name. It was said that they were a law unto themselves and did what they liked when they liked. Mullins tried to see the ends of their swords but they were concealed within cloaks and greatcoats- it was said that they would cut an inch or so from their scabbard and use the bare end of the blade to stab and poke people with while they extricated their belongings. It was said they worked in groups of four to six and they were never caught in the act or brought to justice later on. The worst of it in most people's eyes was that they were all educated and well to do men who had no need to be stealing.

"They may be Dindies" Mullins said finally "but their faces have been seen by all and sundry here now so I doubt if there is anything to go down that they will play any part of it"

"So we have to wait for some masked warriors before we can get excited" Cleaves said.

"Who knows maybe the Liberty Boys or the Ormonde Boys will save him to use in their next street fight" Mullins joked again. As he said this he became aware of a solitary soldier making his way through the crowd and as his eyes followed this man others joined him so that the majority of the crowd was watching him by the time he got to the scaffold and handed an official some paper.

The face of the official- no one actually seemed to know who he was, had up to now been beaming with what many took for pride at the fact that he was in charge of such a momentous execution, dropped and grew sullen as he read the paper. He looked at the soldier but said nothing, it was a look that asked if what was written were really the case and the solder understanding this nodded that it was. The official turned and said something to the hangman and the priest who seemed surprised by what he said. The priest shook his head and blessed himself and the hangman just stood there as though he were contemplating what to do next. The official nodded at the structure of the scaffold to the men who had erected it and they began to gather around it in the unmistakable fashion of preparing for it to be disassembled.

A loud level of conversation then seemed to emerge from the back of the crowd that gathered and those closer to the front wondered if this was the entry of the condemned. It was very confusing for everyone as to what was happening. And then the road went up "Reprieved!" and it spread from mouth to mouth in surprise, anger, shock, confusion, fear and disappointment.

Almost as soon as this was uttered the crowd began to move as one. They passed the burial ground at Merrion Row, the north side of the green off Beaux's walk and then through Reparee Fields before coming through Hell and finally to Cornmarket and the gates of 'The Black Dog.' When they got there, which was only a ten minute walk, their anger at his release was at boiling point and almost everyone among them was willing to do mortal harm to Olocher should he cross their path.

There was a military cordon set up around the gates and the crowd was forced to stop a distance away but not so far that they could not see the gates.

"Where is he?" people cried out. "If you can't supply justice give him to us as we'll supply it ourselves!" "Where is that monster?" "Let us at him!" and then there was suddenly a wave of silence that went from front to back of the crowd.

"What's happenin'" Cleaves asked the taller Mullins from where they stood about thirty men deep. Mullins could see no reason for the silence and he looked at the gates of the prison for a few moments before he noticed that there were some soldiers loading something onto a cart just outside.

"He got a blade in somehow and killed himself last night" one of the soldiers said to clarify that this was indeed the dead body of Thomas Olocher that was being carried away from the prison.

"He's dead!" went up a cry "Done himself in!" said another and once again the news rippled back through the crowd and the emotions and confusions came sprawling forward once again.

"Can't you fuckers even babysit for one night without messing it up!" someone called out at the soldiers.

"Less of that talk" the soldier said back. The crowd was showing signs of becoming restless and the soldiers knew it, had seen it many times before.

The cart began to move off and the crowd surged forward after it.

"Where are they taking him?" they demanded. The soldiers pushed back and the prison guards were also called into duty to help them. An officer who at the gates shouted into the crowd in a loud authoritative voice,

"You are required to disperse at once lest I have to call for troops to disperse you!" but the anger was too much instilled in the blood of the people now and they surged forward and broke through the ranks of the soldiers (the prison guards gave up and stepped out of the way almost immediately) and Brick- who had been at the gates while Olocher was being taken out, ran back inside and had the gates shut quickly.

The officer called for backup but he was quickly silenced with the weight of blows against him and his soldiers too were quickly overrun. The cart had tried to pick up speed when the driver saw what was happening behind but the slick conditions of the road gave the wheels no traction and he too was quickly engulfed by the crowd and pulled from his cart and it was then overturned, Olocher's body wrapped in a white sheet spilling into the sewer runs at the kerbside.

"Best place for him" someone cried and mighty cheer went up.

The body was pulled up by four men who disappeared down an alleyway as the new soldiers arrived and began to fire into the crowds. People scattered in every direction and there were wails of pain as people fell to the ground and were trampled by others escaping the hot flashes of the muskets. Cleaves had grabbed Mullins and ran towards the river, his intention to get to the other side and lay low over there for a time.

They were not far from Cornmarket when it was clear that the soldiers were not in pursuit; at least not in the direction they were running. They had probably just wanted to regain control of the area outside of the prison gates. Cleaves noticed this and he grabbed onto Mullins' arm.

"Stop, stop, they're not coming this way" Mullins stopped and he looked behind.

"No point going over to the northside when we can just go home and lay low there" Cleaves said.

They were in Swan Alley now so they continued onto Merchants Quay and followed the Liffey west to Ushers Quay before turning up Dog and Duck Yard where Mullins lived. They stopped at his door and looked around. There were people scuttling about everywhere and back into their own homes but there was no sign of the soldiers anywhere.

"You should come in and stay the night" Mullins said to Cleaves.

"Sure I'm only a few streets away" Cleaves said "I'll be fine" and he was making to move away when Mullins grabbed his arm.

"Seriously Cleaves, you should come in. Those English bastards will be looking for blood tonight" Cleaves didn't say anything, he looked like he was mulling it over. "You have to go right through them to get home" Mullins said to sway him some more. Cleaves nodded at this was still looked like he was weighing up his chances of getting home unharmed. "Come on, I have a coddle on and enough whiskey to see us through the night" and this was the final sway needed as they both entered through the doorway.

Chapter 5

Thomas Olocher's body was found the following morning on Lesser Elbow Lane in a condition that had even the soldiers who found it (men who had seen the most brutal war had to offer in both India and the West Indies) gagging. The white sheet he had been wrapped in had been taken from him and lay torn muddy and bloody a few feet from the body. They had to shoo some pigs away who had been feasting on the corpse and it was this that made the men nauseous. Olocher's cheeks were gone and the wound at his throat where he had slashed to kill himself had been gnawed at and opened further. The clothes he wore were rags on him as the feral pigs teeth had torn through to get to the flesh underneath.

The filth from the roads and sewers and that which had been on the pigs bodies was all mashed up with torn skin, blood and pig saliva. His intestines had been pulled from his body and this is what the last pig was working on when they got there. A small dog sat to the side with a wet red snout awaiting his turn having been forced out by the much larger and more aggressive animals. What was not red or mud coloured of Olocher's skin was blue white and looked as though it would be hard to the touch. It was not possible to tell if those who took the body had done any injury to it any more.

At the infirmary Alderman James looked over the wreckage of the body. The surgeon had left him alone, leaving gruffly and saying that they should have left the body in the lane for the animals to finish off. James had been at the trial of this man and in fact had been involved in bringing the case to the Magistrate. To look at what was left of him now he could hardly recognise it as the same being. None of Olocher's own victims had ever looked as bad as this when he had finished with them.

He left orders for the body to be disposed of in a proper, albeit quiet, way and he went back to his home on Henrietta Street. The carriage rattled over the uneven road surface and James tried to focus on some papers he had in relation to other crimes reported to him. Thomas Olocher may have been the most notorious of Dublin criminals this season but he was by no means the only one, he was not even the only murderer on the prowl. This was the case he was looking at now, three murders on the north side of Dublin all around Haymarket. This seemed an open and shut case and the guilty party was known to him and would be easy to find if he tried to run. The new worry was the public reaction now; before people were tried and sentenced and that was an end to it but now with all the leaflets that were distributed about each crime and the rumours and stories that spread like wildfire (it had to be said mostly from the higher classes) through the taverns and markets, the public had plenty to say about the justice system and were not afraid to express it. This man, the other murder he thought of now, would have to be tried quickly and hanged just as quickly and with proper arrangements made for where he was to go before and a decent search of his person made this time. Riots were the last thing the Alderman wanted in this ever growing city.

When he got home dinner was about to be served and his guests had arrived before him. He made his apologies and joined them after a quick change of clothes.

Throughout the meal he found that he couldn't stop seeing the body of Thomas Olocher; it was as though it were imprinted in his mind. He'd seen countless dead in his many years and in states of extreme violence at that but none of them had ever had the effect of what he had seen today.

The meat on his table was dripping with grease and gravy and he couldn't help but see the remnants of Olocher's limbs and innards as he looked at the food. Potatoes mashed up looked like the mulch that hid behind the open skull face he'd looked into.

The events of the past twenty four hours were of course well known by now and they were the talk of the table. It never ceased to amaze James how interested people were in gory details and criminal goings on when if ever faced with the reality they would either faint or throw up. He answered their questions with disinterest as though it was all in a day's work and the case was no different to those he generally worked on.

He changed the subject to other crimes frequently only to see it ramble back to the same point it had started.

As he saw his guests out that night he noticed their eyes alight with the first hand gossip and the merriness of drink and for whatever reason he pictured the dog who had been bullied away from the body by the pigs. It had waited patiently around the whole time he was at the body, long after the pigs were gone as though he was going to get another go at it and was just waiting for his opportunity. A hungry dog that was willing to wait, how often did you come across that?

Chapter 6

It was a pitiful night to be on sentry duty. A clear black sky showered stars over the housetops of Dublin and a small crescent moon threw what little illumination it had in its thin band over the sleeping city. The lack of cloud cover was the reason that the temperature was so low and there was a chilling wind that whipped through the streets and alleyways that led to the larger space at Cornmarket and then pressed hard against the walls of 'The Black Dog' and as a consequence against Martin Gleeson who was on sentry at the foot of the south tower that night.

The night had been uneventful so far, just a few men from the whiskey cabins and taverns to send on their way and a couple of street walkers teasing him and offering their services. It was late enough now that Gleeson was not expecting to see anyone until the early morning traders going to set up stalls. This was the worst part of guarding the prison at night; there was nothing to do or see for hours to come yet.

This was a new sentry position that was only used since the mob violence the day Olocher was taken away. The army wanted security standards improved at the prison in case they ever had to place someone there again. Brick protested about finding money to pay for another two guards every night but the rumour was that he was to pay for them himself or the army would make sure his life was a worse hell than it already was.

At about four o'clock in the morning Gleeson was at his most weary and was leaning with his back to the prison walls. Twice his head dropping into sleep had startled him but he felt too tired to stand up straight. That was until he heard a noise coming from one of the thin alleys up the road a little from the prison. He stood erect and looked in the direction of the alley. He couldn't be fully sure that he had heard something, that it had not been the beginning of a dream but he listened closely and then he heard it again.

Then he heard it again, and was sure he heard it this time, a low rolling noise that he couldn't place and yet there was something familiar about it. He listened more intently and stepped out from the wall to see down the street better. Now there was a new noise and this was one he did know, it was the noise of a pig shuffling through the alleys looking for something to eat; he couldn't stop his mind from picturing those pigs eating the body of Olocher a few days ago and what those soldiers must have seen from the description (fifth hand) that he had received. He felt a shiver of fear run through him at the thought and then he heard the other noise again but it was closer now and he recognised it as a growling noise.

The hairs stood up all over his body and he snapped fully awake. His sensible mind knew that it was probably a dog trying to warn the pig he heard off from whatever little food it had found but the images he had just conjured up of Olocher and the pigs brought fresh images of all kinds of beasts coming at him from the darkness. The noise again, echoing off the cobbled street and stone walls, no mistaking it for anything other than an animalistic growl now, and again it seemed to be closer. Gleeson gripped his short halberd more firmly and glanced around to see if there was anyone around but there was not.

Cold sweat gathered on his back causing him to shudder at the shock of it and he stood facing where the noises came from; his feet rigid to the spot where he stood and his ears cocked for any sound. A tremendous bark and injured howl of a dog peeled off as a midsized black canine flew from the darkness past him and into the streets beyond and then once again he heard the pig he knew he had and what he heard was the noise of a pig snuffling and eating something. His sensible mind was right all along.

He released his tense grip on the halberd and he could feel the sweat now under his armpits from holding so tight. He stepped back to the wall and leaned against it and he smiled at his silliness, his letting his imagination get the better of him and...

"RAAAAARH!" something big and black came at him from that same darkness he had peered into. The massive bulk knocked him to the ground and then all he could see was furious eyes over a long black snout before massive white teeth starting slashing into him; the monsters jaws seeming to be able to work independently of one another, their size and ferocity startling him and hurting him in equal measure. Gleeson screamed and tried to fight back but he was badly hurt and there was nothing he could seem to do, all of his strength seemed to be taken up by his knees as he tried to force his attacker away from him. He felt a scorching pain across his cheek and then in the opposite direction he felt another across his neck as the teeth slashed at him 'He's trying to bite my head off!' was the last thought he had before losing consciousness and as he drifted away he heard someone shouting somewhere from high up but what they said he didn't know.

Had he stayed conscious he would have been aware of the other guards rallying to his point. One from inside the towers had seen that there was something going on but what he was at a loss to say. He had called down and upon hearing the cries of pain from Gleeson he had sounded the alert.

The women in the 'Nunnery' had heard the attack from their low street level windows though they had been too frightened to go to it and look out. Kate listened to the sounds of shredding clothes and flesh and she heard the vicious snarling of whatever it was that attacked the guard.

When they pulled his tattered and torn body inside the gates of the prison and slammed them shut behind, the women could see the bloody mess that was Gleeson. Kate let out a howl of fear and revulsion just as Brick appeared once more in the movement of agitated dressing.

"Keep low in there or you'll go hungry again tarts!" he shouted in with a quick angry glance. Kate was silent then as she watched him rush up to the other guards and break through to see what was going on.

"What the hell happened?" he asked of the guards standing there tending the victim.

"Something attacked him at the south tower sentry point.

"What do you mean something? Who attacked him?" Brick shouted

"I was up in the north tower and I heard something outside. When I looked down there was something big and black over him and it was doing savage damage to him" one of the guards who had come down the winding stairs said, his face white with what he had seen.

"A man in all black you say? What weapon was he using to do this?" The guard who had seen the attack looked at some of the others as though for support.

"It didn't look like a man sir" he said "and I didn't see any weapon" Brick looked at him suspiciously,

"Have you been drinking?" he whispered harshly at him and pulled him forward to smell his breath,

"No sir!" the guard exclaimed in a wounded tone.

"Where's the doctor" Brick called out now letting go of the guard.

"On the way sir" another of the guards answered.

As Kate looked out now she could see that they were all at a loss as to what to do with the injured man while they waited. She could no longer see him but there was a pool of blood forming on the floor and she could hear guttural sounds as though he were trying to breath and there was blood sloshing about in his lungs or his throat. He was moaning on and off as well in a delirious way and she could hear his feet scrape on the floor as he writhed about. She felt terribly sorry for him and wondered if he would not be dead before the doctor even got here.

"Can you not do something to make him a bit more comfortable?" she asked through the bars, "try to stop him bleeding maybe?" The guards looked at her and it was clear in each of their eyes that they would do something if they didn't think they would only make him feel worse.

"I told you to shut up in there!" Brick shouted at them. Kate backed away from the cell door and back into the folds of the women who were just behind here.

"Better not say anything more" Betty whispered to her "the doctor will be here soon and he'll do what he can"

Soon they heard the clipping of a horse outside and they heard a man dismount and the gates rattle to a heavy knock. The wooden gates pulled open and the noise was terrific now in opposition to the silence that had fallen over the prison for the last ten minutes. The doctor rushed in and he saw the man straight away and knelt by his side examining him. He pulled a handkerchief from his coat and pressed it against the neck of the maimed man.

"Why did nobody stem the bleeding?" he asked looking admonishingly at the people who stood around him. No one answered and the doctor looked back to the patient.

"What happened to him?" the doctor asked.

"He was attacked outside on sentry duty"

"Attacked by what?" the doctor asked examining the wounds on the man's chest causing him to cry out in pain. Brick looked at the guards and then replied

"We don't know, we heard him cry out and we found him like this"

"Some of these wounds look like they were done by an animal, a large dog or something but then there bruises here have points like those you would see from a hoofed animal wound" the doctor said pointing out things as he spoke.

Kate trembled at the idea that an animal had done this to the man and she looked at the bars on the windows and wondered if it might be possible for it to get in through them to her. This basement dungeon took a terrible toll on the mind she felt. She had been here only six days but it had felt like an eternity and every night there were new fears of what could come and get her in this dark and stinking pit. She scolded herself in daylight hours for her wild thoughts at night. She would seek out the corners and crannies that were in complete darkness once the sun went down and she would see that there were nothing in those spaces, that in a lot of cases there could be nothing in them but then again at night those same dark spots would fill her with terror and she would feel that something was watching her from there and waiting for her to let her guard down.

She was reasonable with herself and she could only curse the fact that her first time in a prison was the time that Olocher had been sentenced and she was there on the night that he killed himself. She remembered the pigs squealing at the gates that night and when she heard the doctor say that there were bruises in the shapes of hoofed feet she wondered for a moment if the guard had been attacked by a pig but the thought seemed ridiculous to her; the idea of one of those lazy slothful animals attacking a man seemed wild to her, and the fact that there were the teeth marks of a different animal type also swayed her back to her senses.

"Take this man to the infirmary and make sure to keep this pressed to his neck" the doctor said rising and exchanging places with one of the guards.

"Will he live?" Brick asked the doctor after taking his arm and leading him a little away from the victim's ears. The doctor looked at him and then back at Brick,

"It will be touch and go" he said "I won't be surprised to see him dead in the morning but I've seen men survive worse"

Chapter 7

Mary Sommers was the only known person to have witnessed any of Thomas Olocher's crimes. Her tearful testimony and her fingering of Olocher as the murderer of her aunt were instrumental in his being sentenced to death. Many thought that it was the fact that she had seen him slash his own legs in frenzy during the attack that had sealed Olocher's fate. When the trial was over Olocher gave her a menacing look before he was led away to the 'Black Dog' prison at Newgate. She had felt that same fear she had felt when trapped in that closet while he butchered her aunt; she was breathless every time she faced him in the courtroom and even when she thought about him or heard his name mentioned she could feel the restriction of breath in her lungs and throat. She often felt while lying down to sleep that he was on top of her clutching her throat and using his weight to cave in her chest. When the trial was over she was thanked for her bravery and testimony and was let out to fend for herself.

When she went back to where she had lived with her aunt the landlord asked if she had any money. She didn't and when she told him this he said that he was very sorry for everything that had happened to her and her aunt but that she was going to have to leave in a week's time if she could not start earning enough to pay the rent on the room. Mary was devastated and she spent that whole night crying.

She had never worked before and she knew how to do nothing of any value. When she asked the landlord what she could do he simply shrugged and said that she was a clever girl and that she would figure it out. She felt she was a clever enough girl but that didn't translate into anything she could think of to do. For two days she barely left the room she rented only going out for small bits of food. What little money she had could only go on food for now and she knew that it was going to run out much sooner rather than later no matter how little she thought she could get by on without starving.

She finally got the idea to go to the coffee houses, tea houses and taverns to see if she could do any tidying or cleaning. Though she was pretty and pleasant she found that these places were oversubscribed with girls like her looking for work. One tavern said that their previous women had become ill and that she would fill this post for the time being but the hours were late into the evening and the pay was lower than she expected. She accepted though as she knew that even if she was put out onto the streets she would need every penny she could make to feed herself.

As she went to look for other work at various butchers, milliners and other trade businesses she met Sarah, a woman who was formerly a friend of her now deceased aunt and Sarah was able to secure her some work assisting in the market at Temple Bar and also as a street vendor for selling potatoes when one of the normal women couldn't make it to work- (which it turned out was a lot) she would have to give half what she made though to the woman whose position she had taken. This didn't seem fair but she was told that this was the common practice and that if she didn't like it she didn't have to do the work at all and then she would get nothing.

This was all unreliable work and by the end of the week, though she had done well to make anything at all, she was in no position to be able to afford to stay where she had lived for as long as she could remember. And so on a cold October morning she walked the city with her bag over her shoulder and tears in her eyes not having a notion as to where she was going to stay that night.

After doing this for some time she found herself down by the river and she saw the trade ships lined up along the banks and others in midstream waiting to dock and she wondered if she might get onto one of them and get away from this place, get to somewhere warm where she wouldn't need a roof over her head or clothes to keep her warm but again the fantasy was short lived, she knew nothing of other places or languages and would be as bad off anywhere as here with no money in her pockets.

As she looked out at the grey light over the river she was lost in thought of the food and clothes that were probably being loaded and unloaded for transit to England and beyond.

She huddled against the walled banks as it was acting as a buffer against the biting wind that whipped the quays today. It must have been the third time her name was said that she registered someone was addressing her.

"Mary love?" she tuned to find Sarah peering into her face. "Have you been crying dear? What's the matter?" Mary found she couldn't speak just then and the tears came again as she fell into the welcoming arms of the older woman's embraces.

"What is it Mary?" she asked after giving the girl a time to compose herself.

"I was put out of my room today"

"And you have nowhere else you can go?" asked Sarah. Mary shook her head in sorrow and began to cry again. Sarah soothed her and rubbed her back "Now, now little girl, you can't be crying so much over a small thing like this" she said. Mary was shocked and she stopped crying, pulling back so as to be able to see Sarah's face.

"A little thing!" she almost cried out.

"Look around you Mary" Sarah said gesturing in a circle "Almost everyone you can see has had nights where there was nowhere to stay, you are lucky to have made it to your age before it happened to you for the first time"

"What am I supposed to do?" Mary asked "What do people normally do?"

"You can stay with me for tonight. That will get you started and then we can try to sort something out for you" Sarah said and almost before she was finished speaking Mary had grabbed her in an embrace and thanking her in the most effusive manner she could.

"Thank you so much, I'll pay you" she said.

"Don't get too excited Mary, this is only for tonight, there are eight of us living where I do already. You will still have to get something sorted for yourself"

"Ok" Mary said and then she wondered what she could do to sort this for herself. She was going to have to find some people to live with. It Sarah had to live with seven other people she was going to have to live with at least as many as Sarah made more money than she did by a long way.

"Spend the day looking for something love. I'll meet you back here at 7 O'clock ok?" Sarah said and she scuttled off towards the unloading ships.

Chapter 8

Alderman James sat in the large spacious dining room at his home on Henrietta Street. He was alone at the table now, his guests for today having gone back to work or home, and he picked absent mindedly at the now cold neck of mutton that had formed part of dinner. He was in foul temper and was glad that his guests were gone; once again they had brought up his 'heroics' at the time of one of the weavers riots up in the Liberties. That event held nothing but regret for him now and earned him the sobriquet that he knew well now of 'Alderman Level Low.'

It was no secret in the city what had happened. Dublin's weavers had fallen on hard times (it was actually weavers from all over the country as well who flocked to Dublin and made the crisis there worse than it already was) there had been a collapse in the wool market and the new fashion for Indian made garments and flashy French silk had put countless numbers of them out of work. Things had become so bad that the underemployed weavers began to engage in riotous behaviours. They would accost people in the streets and tear their clothes if they were made of foreign materials, they would even stop the carriages of the upper classes and many women had exquisite fine dresses torn and shredded by them. The result was often violence and soon the weavers were attacking the very shops who sold the evil materials or goods with them as part of their manufacture.

On the particular day of Alderman James' 'heroics' the agitated weavers had gone further than before in the rioting and many people were injured and scarred by their liberal blade strokes. A gentleman of the upper classes was pulled from his carriage and dragged through the grime at the side of the road by a group of these men and he was brought to the Liberties where they stripped him naked, painted his body with warm tar and took turns applying feathers to him.

When Alderman James arrived with the soldiers the man was in a delirious state and was wandering around as though insane. The weavers were nearby fighting with other business owners and James ordered the soldiers to fire a volley of powder at the group in the hope of ending the violence but this behaviour was perceived as leniency and an unwillingness to shoot at them for real and the weavers began to hurl stones at the soldiers. James ordered live shot to be used for a second volley but the soldiers fired above the heads of the rioters and were again met with boos and a barrage of stones. James ordered another live shot volley and this time as the men aimed above the heads of the rioters he used his staff to lower the barrels of the soldiers who then discharged into the crowd killing some and wounding others. This had the desired effect and the rioters fled in all directions to escape.

James knew why he had done what he did that day; there was no other choice, he had to maintain order and that was the only recourse left to him that day, but he felt terrible about it even as he was lowering the barrel of the first soldier's musket. And it had gotten worse every day since then. His friends and peers think of this as a heroic act and one that saved much worse rioting in the long run and they never seemed to fail to remind him of it no matter how many years had passed since that day.

Alderman James had wanted to do something to make up for what he had done ever since and it was only when it was pointed out to him by the mayor himself that James had become very lenient in his disbursement of punishments for crimes in his district that he had for the sake of his career to start harsher punishments in line with the other Aldermen and magistrates. The only visible symbol of regret he showed was that he had all his clothes (as much a practicable) made from wool by local weavers, but he alone was not going to revive that dying industry.

There was a knock of the door.

"Enter" he said without enthusiasm. A man of about five feet ten inches entered in fine clothes with a glistening scabbard holding his sword, the handle of which was adorned with some jewels of azure colour.

"Mr Edwards!" James said in surprise

"Something has happened in the Liberties" Edwards said seriously. James stood up, he was about the same height as this man but he was a much meatier figure with thick shoulders and neck against Edwards' more refined and thin shape. Both had the same colour almost black hair. James poured a drink and handed it to Edwards without asking if he wanted one and beckoned for him to sit down.

"What is it Mr. Edwards?"

"Two nights ago there was an attack on one of the guards over at Newgate" Edwards said.

"Yes I know, some men roughed him up trying to secure the release of their friend. Drunken idiots" James said.

"That is what I had heard originally myself Alderman" Edwards said with a sly smile cloying his face.

"And now you have heard something different?"

"Very different" There was a silence.

"Don't go silent on me Mr. Edwards! What did you hear?" The Alderman said in exasperation. Edwards smiled still more and James knew that it was something good he had. He paused and studied the man's face for clues to what he wanted.

"What will it cost me this time?"

"Not a thing" Edwards replied practically beaming now.

"Then what?"

"Well maybe you can make sure that there are no soldiers in the vicinity of Hell on Sunday night next" Edwards said nonchalantly.

"Why?"

"Nothing illegal as such but you know the soldiers, they just get involved with everything they see and cause trouble where there really isn't any"

"Are the Pinking Dindies planning to burn down another brothel?" James asked with a raised eyebrow.

"I couldn't tell you what they are up to but my reason has nothing to do with them" Edwards said, "and to be fair Darkey Kelly was a murderess after all" he added.

"How do I know what you have is worth my turning a blind eye to whatever it is you have planned?"

"It is, I can assure you of that. If what I have heard is true it is exactly what you have been looking for" James could sense Edward had him over a barrel. "Listen what's going to happen on Sunday is the settling of a bet. It will be rambunctious and noisy for a little but that is the true extent of it" James mulled this over before answering.

"Fine, now tell me what you have heard"

"That a guard of the debtor's prison was attacked, and savagely I might add, is true but he was not attacked by drunken louts trying to free a friend"

"Then who attacked him?" James was getting annoyed at the playing around the issue.

"Not who Alderman, but what attacked him"

"What do you mean?"

"I have it on good authority from three different eyewitnesses that the guard was attacked by some wild beast that did ferocious damage to the man"

"What beast and what good authority?"

"One of the other guards of the prison, one of the people who was incarcerated there that evening and the victim himself"

"The victim said he was attacked by a wild beast?"

"Yes and I am afraid it was the last thing he said"

"He died today?"

"This morning, first thing, just after I spoke to him"

"And what animal are we talking about, a feral dog?"

"It doesn't sound like a dog from his description but then it doesn't sound like any animal by his description" Edwards said sighing and sipping from his tumbler.

"What did the witnesses say?"

"The guard says he saw something very big and black on top of the man but he also could name no animal"

"And the other?"

"I am afraid that person only heard the attack and they couldn't put a name to animal they heard either"

"So what do you think it was ?"

"I don't know to be honest but it did remind of something ghastly I heard years ago"

"Which was what?"

"I once heard that a pack of wolves driven mad by hunger got inside the city walls of Paris, this was back in the 1400s I think"

"And?"

"Well, they were starving and naturally they killed people and ate them" there was a glint in Edwards' eyes that was almost lupine and it sent a shiver through James. Edwards was the man to go to for information about anything that was unseemly or morbid but how much he knew and how much he told were probably two very different things James mused as he looked at this almost evil, mocking face.

"So you think it's a wolf?" he asked bluntly, not willing to engage in ghost stories or mystical talk.

"As I say, I don't know but the doctor who examined the man said there the marks from large teeth on the body, face and neck of the man that would indicate a large animal like a wolf"

"Did the doctor say anything else about what it could have been?"

"Yes actually" and again that smile, "he said that it looked like there were hoof marks on his chest"

"Hoofmarks?"

"Yes, that doesn't' add up with the teeth though" and at this Edwards stood, "unless the Devil has large sharp teeth and in that case he's our man!" and at this he laughed out loud.

"I wish you wouldn't speak so flippantly of the Devil" James said also standing up.

"I'm sure he doesn't mind it"

"I wasn't saying for his sake"

"Well Alderman James, until we meet again" Edwards said holding out a hand which James took. "If there is an animal out there it may well do this again, even if it doesn't if you are the one to find it and capture it you may get a new name that better fits your sensibilities"

"Keep me posted on anything else you find out Mr. Edwards"

"I will and don't forget, no soldiers in Hell from about 9 O'clock on Sunday night?"

"I won't forget"

Edwards went to leave but he stopped at the door and turned back to James.

"Seriously though Alderman, be careful. I know I speak lightly of these things but the fact is an animal of some description has killed a man and there is no reason why it wouldn't be able to do the same to you"

"Yes it would be a shame if you had to get into the secrets and fears of a new Alderman altogether and learn how to bribe him" James smiled though there was nothing friendly in it.

"Don't be silly Alderman, if you were gone I'd just see to it that whoever I wanted to would become your successor" and he laughed out loud again, nodding as he left the room and James could hear him laughing all the way down the hallway to the front door.

When he was finally gone James went to the window and looked out into the dark of the evening. He could feel the cold from outside through the glass pane and he wondered what had happened a few nights ago at the debtor's prison. He imagined himself at Corn Market with the body of a wolf dead at his feet and the gratitude of the people of the Liberties. What would they call him then? Something humorous no doubt but also just as likely to incorporate his current nickname as his real name. He never understood where the wit of these people came from and he could predict nothing of what might be said in jest about any event that transpired.

If he could do this, get to the bottom of what did this to that poor man he would go some ways he felt towards redeeming himself but even as he thought these fantastic thoughts he felt that he was destined to be Alderman Level Low for life.

Alderman Lupine Low, he mused and this brought a smile to his face and stepped back from the window and filled his drink again.

Chapter 9

Kate woke from yet another nightmare. She could smell immediately that she was still in the dungeon of the 'Black Dog.' She leaned up a little and as was her habit after these nightmares of the last few nights she looked out the window expecting to see something evil wanting to get in, something menacing and glowering that only wanted her. Her eyes saw nothing and she glanced at the black spaces in the room. The syrupy residue of the nightmare, screaming pigs and the screaming guard, was thick on her forehead and temples and she could smell the pungent sweat that soaked her clothes and the smell of the damp hay they lay on.

She lay looking at the ceiling which was alive with reflected surface water from the floor; it looked so clean and beautiful she couldn't believe it . She followed the patterns that it made as she tried to rid herself of the uneasy feelings that were inside of her. This place was getting to her, there was no doubt of that. She hadn't thought she'd be here so long but obviously no one was willing to pay for her to get out.

The uneasiness refused to lift and a half hour later she was still a bag of nerves and almost sick to her emptier than usual stomach. None of the others were awake and they seemed to be coping with things here much better than she, but then they had been here many times before. Some of the women in the brothel talked of this place with bravado and joked about their times in here but for Kate it was never going to be anything but a living nightmare for her to think of this place and she would live in constant fear now of ever being out back in here. She heard a low grumble and wondered whose belly it was of the sleeping others. It wasn't hers because she didn't feel anything.

She was looking at the ceiling again when the grumble went again only it was louder this time and more like a growl. Kate smiled at this; it was one those things that just seemed funny when you were the only awake at three in the morning or whatever time it was.

When she heard it again she was no longer smiling and a sense of terror sprang up through her entire body. It wasn't one of the others hungry stomach, it was coming from outside. She stayed still and as silent as possible. She watched the window from her prone position and then she heard it again, a low growl and much closer this time. She was petrified and she began to cry, slapping her hand over her mouth to stop any noise that might involuntarily emit from her.

She wanted to wake the others as was natural to share her fear but she forced herself not to, that would cause a disturbance and perhaps draw the creature towards them. She was rocking a little now from crying and she tensed up to try to stop herself, some of the others were beginning to stir a little.

Tears were streaming over her fingers now as the next growl was so close it had to becoming from just outside the window, just outside what she was able to see. She could hear it as it sniffed the air and she was sure that it would catch hold of the smells emanating from her that she had herself smelled. There was another low growl and then the true horror happened for her. She saw the dark shape move past the window, she couldn't help but yelp a little in fear but the creature didn't stop but instead just passed on towards Back Lane direction.

When she could no longer hear it she got up quietly and went to the door of the cage. She was almost hysterical with tears now as she said to the guard in a forced whisper,

"It's outside again!" He startled awake from a sleep she didn't even know he had been having.

"What?" he said in confusion

"The thing that attacked the guard the other night" she said louder now, "it's outside now!" He jumped up and called softly to the guard on the inside of the gates.

"Any sign of anything outside?" The other guard looked out and then back shaking his head.

"Nothing I can see"

"Can you see Jeremiah?" the first asked and the second looked out again.

"No" The first guard then called up the stairs,

"Watch out for Jeremiah outside. Can you see him" A few seconds later a voice came back,

"No sign!"

Kate watched as the first guard went to the gate and said to the guard there,

"Open up and we'll have a quick look out" The gate creaked open a little and the first guard stuck his head out far enough to see both ways. "No sign" he said looking back inside. He stepped outside and called the missing guards name quietly but enough to be heard in the silent streets. Then she heard the one now outside say "I think I see something, wait here a moment" and she heard him walking a little away from the gates and in the direction the beast had gone.

"Don't go out there alone!" she called out and now the other women did stir and sat up with sleepy heads and imbecilic visages.

"Quiet in there" the one on the gate called over.

"That creature is out there, don't let him go out alone! He'll be killed!"

"What are you saying Kitty?" the women asked her.

"I saw it pass the window, it was growling outside and then it went off up the laneway"

"What was it?" they asked

"I don't know but it was all black and it growled and sniffed the air right at that window"

Just then there was a call from outside,

"At the walls, at the walls outside, Back Lane!" Some guards came running down the stairs and out through the gate. Somebody was shouting directions from the tower and the women grew afraid of what was going on.

In a few minutes, with guards coming and going all the while the first guard came in with a white face. He was carrying an extra halberd and something else in his arms which he placed on the ground. Brick arrived again in his now usual manner, agitated and barely dressed,

"Can't I get one night decent sleep in this fuckin' place?" he thundered "What is it now?" He came into the opening and he saw as Kate did now, that it was a pile of bloody and torn clothes that had been brought back from outside.

"What's this?" Brick asked

"This is all there was left of him sir"

"Who?"

"Jeremiah sir, he was on outside duty tonight, there's blood all over the ground just up the lane and this is all that was left" said the guard who had gone out first.

Chapter 10

Edwards was drunk and in high spirits when the appointed hour finally came that Sunday evening. A boy had been sent to scout the local area and he reported that there were no soldiers in Hell or any of the streets just off it. James had kept his word so, Edwards thought. They boy was highly excited and Edwards clipped him on the back of the head and told him to go and keep watch out on the streets.

His horse was getting very uncomfortable but this was only going to aid things; it had been extremely agitated when they had forced it up the two flights of stairs and into this long room. The drunken members of the Hellfire Club had not been able to contain their merriment and there was much laughter as they pushed and heaved and whipped the frightened animal that had never been inside anything tighter than a spacious barn before.

"The soldiers are gone" Edwards announced to the rest of them who cheered and raised their glasses.

"Get on with it then!" someone shouted.

"Patience brother, the carriage is not in place yet" said Edwards. A few men went to the large window and looked down at the street just as a pristine black carriage rounded the corner. It came up and stopped in the centre of the road in front of the building they were in. The driver looked up and doffed his hat in a theatrical manner, clearly inebriated as well, and they all cheered down to him.

"Will this spot do?" he called up. A man came up to the window and looked down and then looked to Edwards and nodded.

"That'll do it" he said in a gruff manner and Edwards made motion to the driver that it was.

"Well Gentlemen" he then said addressing the room "I for one will want to see this from street level. Any of you are of course welcome to stay up here but I think it will be better down there" and he made his way to the door with the majority of the men following.

"You still want to make this wager?" the gruff man asked him with an evil smile to which Edwards returned a much more pleasant one,

"I supply the horse and the carriage and you do the rest"

"Well it's your money to do with what you will Edwards"

"I'll see you when you land" Edwards said and he laughed as did most of the men in the room.

When they were down on the street Edwards looked up and down to be sure there were still no soldiers and then shouted up to the room they had been in,

"Whenever you are ready" As he looked up at the candlelit room he realised how high it actually was and he was sure that he was going to win his wager. No one in their right mind would do this. But then who among them right now was in his right mind; they had been drinking since daybreak and it was now almost 10 o'clock at night. As he pondered this there was suddenly an almighty series of crashes as the windows of the second floor were smashed apart from within and then huge shards dashed noisily on the ground nearby. The horses that stood with the carriage jumped and moved away in fright but the driver sat back down and managed to bring them back under control.

When this stopped the streets of Dublin had never seemed quieter. There were a few faces appearing at windows but they quickly disappeared at the sight of well-dressed gentlemen on the street. If it had been a normal night the soldiers would have arrived by now but there was no sound of the stomping march of their boots.

The next sound to be heard was the whinnying of the horse up there in the room, the sound seemed to filter out and echo around the street and they could hear the rider trying to get control of the animal with whips and curses and they heard the sound of furniture breaking and glassware getting knocked over. The hooves on the wooden floor clapped and scraped and then finally there was a final "Yah!" a whipping noise and a massive outburst of neighing from the horse and suddenly the beast sprang from the window jamb and out into the night air.

As they looked up in amazement; no one had thought it would actually happen, both horse and rider seemed frozen in the air, both with masks of the utmost terror. The sweat glistened on the black coat of the horse and small shards of glass twinkled in candle and moonlight as all plummeted to the earth.

"Look out!" someone shouted and then the men realised that having not thought it would happen they had not given themselves a safe distance to watch from. Drunken men scurried everywhere and the smiling driver quickly lost his jocularity as he saw that the horse was about to land on the carriage, he leaped clear and ended up covered in street grime just as the rear legs of the horse hit the top of the carriage. The rider was sent flailing through the air and landed with a sickening thud against the building across the street from where they had leapt. The horse let loose a final screech as its head dashed against the cobbles and it was killed instantly; a loud cracking of broken legs happening just after it had died.

The men rushed to the rider and found that he was alive but delirious with pain. His leg was snapped at the shin and the ragged bone protruded through the skin. His body was covered in scrapes and cuts and he felt like jelly as the men picked him to take him to the doctor.

"Wait!" he said when he got a little of his sense back "Edwards" he called. Edwards came to him,

"What is it?"

"Sorry about the carriage, didn't intend for that to happen" the injured man said. Edwards looked at the cracked and splintered top of the carriage and smiled,

"Don't worry about that" he said looking back at the rider, "it was worth it to see that display you utter madman!"
The rider smiled back,

"Never bet against a Hellfire member" he said. Edwards nodded and the men carried the rider off as he lost consciousness.

Edwards was now alone on the street and he surveyed the damage, the glass everywhere, the smashed up carriage and the huge dead horse. The carriage driver was nowhere to be seen, he had probably got caught up in the group taking the rider away and was now drinking somewhere no doubt.

"So this is why you didn't want the soldiers here tonight eh?" a voice said from the darkness.
"You don't have to hide Alderman" Edwards said looking into the darkness.
"Call me James"
"As you wish, James" James came from the shadows and surveyed the scene with Edwards.
"What the hell was this all about anyway?" he asked
"Just a friendly wager"
"That man jumped out of a building on a horse, over a carriage for a wager?" James was astounded.
"Why else would a person do something like that?" Edwards asked amused at James' shock.
"How did it even come about?"
"When you mix alcohol with anything you can be very surprised as to what will arise" Edwards laughed.
"Well this caper has cost somebody a pretty penny, look at that carriage, and that horse looks like it was worth quite a bit"
"Oh well, sometimes you win and sometimes you lose" Edwards said with a resigned sigh and then he looked about as though he were bored and hoping to see something else that might amuse him. "What has you over this side of the city tonight anyway?" he asked the Alderman.
"I'm looking for whatever did those two guards in at Newgate" he replied.
"And you come alone?" Edwards asked "Brave or silly I don't know?"
"Have you heard anything more about it?"
"Nothing solid, there are obviously rumours going around"
"Such as?"

"Just what I have already told you, a large dog, a wolf, things like that" and then at this he chuckled as if remembering something funny.

"What is it?" Alderman asked.

"I just remembered that there is also a rumour that the wooden carving of the devil at the archway there has been leaving his perch at night doing these things" and he laughed out loud this time. This didn't amuse James and he looked towards the arch in question nervously. It was too dark to be able to see if the statue was there or not, the lantern that was there was not lit at the moment.

"I'm going into the Liberties to a walk around by the prison" James said as confidently as he could, "Would you like to join me?"

"Yes why not, I've had enough of those fellows for one day" Edwards said and they set off in the direction of the arch.

As they approached it James could feel the fear growing inside him and he became convinced that the carving would not be there when they passed underneath the arch. He did his best not to show any outward signs of his fear but Edwards was not paying attention to him anyway and he passed through the arch without even glancing in the direction of the carving. James followed through and he did look and there was a wave of relief as he saw that it was indeed where it always had been.

This was another of those Irish sense of humour things that he didn't get. Here was this area adjacent to the grounds of Christ Church and the locals had decided to call the place Hell and put up an idol of the Devil at its entrance way, and every single person here as afraid of the Devil as he was. It beggars belief.

They took a circuitous route that brought them down Cook Street and around by Wormwood, up John Street, across to Vicar Street, then took Swift's Alley to Francis Street and came to Corn Market through Cutpurse. They didn't speak on the way and they watched the lives of the people they passed; men coming out of taverns, women who were probably prostitutes, children hiding and running who probably didn't have any where to stay. It was grim to walk here after ten on a Sunday evening.

When they were finally standing outside the gates of the prison they could feel the eyes of the guards on them, more eyes than they could see they felt sure.

"Poor lads" Edwards said, "They must be terrified that they will be next"

"Probably" James agreed. He was looking at the walls of the prison and looked at where the first guard had been mauled and then they walked a little up Back Lane to where the torn, shredded and bloodied remains of the second guard were found.

"They've stopped patrolling from without the walls of the prison" James said though he knew that Edwards would already know this.

"Seems sensible considering what has happened" he replied. James bent down and he examined the wall where the second guards clothes and halberd had been found, there were blood splashes on the wall that had not been cleaned up.

"It seems reasonable that the attacker came from the lanes of the City Market" James mused nodding across the thin lane to an even thinner alley just across from where they stood.

"Maybe" Edwards nodded in half agreement.

"Maybe?"

"Yes"

"Why only maybe?" James pressed.

"Well, you and everyone else who is looking into this seem to always assume that it was an animal that walks and uses the street and lanes the way that we do but look at these walls, look at all those sections where brick is missing or at all the window ledges and low walls everywhere" Edwards said gesturing at an example of each thing as he said it.

"I see! You know you're right, an animal is much more agile and dexterous than we are. I have been seeing things very narrowly indeed!" James said in revelation.

"An attack from above would indicate why two men, supposedly on alert as guards would have been able to be subdued without the opportunity to fight back in any way"

Though not intended at all James again received an image of the carving of the Devil and he saw it swoop down on the men and he heard their screams as it slashed wildly at them. He shuddered.

"Cold?" Edwards asked.

"Yes, I think a quick walk around a couple more streets and I will be on my way home"

"I'll stay with you until you get to the river and then I'll say goodnight"

They walked a little more through more of the smaller lanes and alleys and then across larger streets and into the area of Ushers Quay. They came across many dogs, cats and pigs but none that looked likely to be their savage beast. They interrupted a few men using the services of street walkers and woke a few who were passed out drunk. They came out along the banks of the black Liffey and looked at some of the ships moored for the night. They teetered slowly.

"Of course it's always possible that it is some kind of animal not native to this land" Edwards said nodding towards the ships. "It could have come in as a stowaway on a one of those and no one would have a clue as to what it was if they say it"

"That's true" James nodded, "but I hope it's not right. At the moment I like the idea that it might be a hungry wolf that has made its way into the city"

"Well I still think that is what makes most sense" Edwards agreed.

"The trouble is that sense doesn't hold much sway when people are afraid" James said. They walked along the quays in thought and said goodnight at Essex Bridge.

Chapter 11

The lock of the cell door clanked and the hinges sang with a high whine when the guard brought in the bread that morning. He handed it out to the queuing women one by one but when it came to Kate's turn he stopped,

"None for you today" he said and nudged her out of the way. The woman next in line stopped as though unsure what she should do.

"Why, what did I do?" Kate cried out.

"You didn't do nothin you stupid cow, you're getting out this mornin'" he said to and he poked the break at the next woman in line who took it happily now that she knew she wasn't betraying anyone.

"How come?" Kate asked but she regretted asking as quickly as it left her mouth.

"Who cares missy, don't question it" the guard said with a half-smile.

It was sunny though very cold when she was let out at just after 9 o' clock. She had lost the coat she had been wearing when the Parish Watch hauled her in and the clothes she wore were so damp from the cell and her sweat that a chill ran through her almost at once and she felt that she was going to be coming down with a cold before the day was out. She looked about but there was no one she knew waiting for her, she hadn't expected there to be. She saw the huge blacksmith from the corner pass by carrying heavy bags of various metal items. He didn't look back at her and she was able to study the scar on his face in the bright sunlight as he passed by.

She began to walk briskly towards her lodgings when a carriage pulled up to block her path. She looked up annoyed and the door swung open.

"In you come out of that cold" Mr Edwards said to her smiling. She knew him and she jumped in straight away sitting across from him. He gave her a blanket and she wrapped it around her.

"You got me out?" she asked looking at him and shivering. He nodded.

"I have been busy for a few weeks but when I went to the House you were nowhere to be found, they told me you were in Newgate"

"Thanks" she said "I couldn't take much more of that place"

"I shouldn't imagine you could, you look and smell terrible" Edwards said with a look almost of revulsion on his face. She knew how she looked and how she smelled but she was still hurt by his saying this. She blushed and looked out at the busy morning street. "You were in there for a week?" he said then.

"Yeah, I think so"

"The night they brought Olocher in?" he asked. The name was unpleasant to hear.

"The night before that" He nodded and then looked out the window himself. She gazed up at him and she wondered if he was drunk. She had often seen him and his friends go all day and all night with alcohol. "Where are you taking me?" she asked noticing that they were going in the direction of neither her home nor the brothel.

"I'm taking you to my house, you can get yourself cleaned up and have a decent sleep and something to eat"

"I have no clothes with me"

"I'll get one of my servants to run out and get you something"

"Why are you doing this for me?" she asked. He had used her services at the brothel many times and he had even brought her out in his carriage (not this one though she noticed) once or twice but he had never shown any interest in her that didn't involve sex before.

"I have some questions about the prison so think of all this as payment for your cooperation"

She saw that they had crossed the river and she was amazed at some of the houses they were now passing. The streets here seemed to be much cleaner and there wasn't anything like the bustle of Hell or the Liberties here. She could see inside some of the houses and there were fantastic candle chandeliers with some kind of ornate glass pieces hanging from them. She could see thick velvet curtains and she imagined how warm these houses must be in the evenings.

Finally the carriage came to a halt and Edwards jumped out and closed the door behind him.

"Take her in by the servant's entrance" she heard him say to the driver and the carriage started up again. It was only two minutes before they arrived at the back door of the house. She got out and went to the door indicated by the driver and she was met in the hallway by a maid who looked her over once and said.

"Follow me"

She did and she was amazed at almost everything she saw. She knew that Mr. Edwards had money but she had no idea how much! Everything seemed to be gold plated or painted luxurious white. The floors had thick carpets her feet sank into that she imagined would be more comfortable to sleep on than any bed she had ever been in. The same beautiful chandeliers were here too hung from the roof of every room and hall she could see into. She came to a fabulous stairway and she could smell the wax used to keep the bannister rails looking pristine, she put her hand on the rail and she had never felt anything to be so smooth and sturdy.

When they reached the first landing the maid brought her into a room and she was once more amazed by what she saw. It was a bedroom with a huge bed covered in blankets and pillows and surrounded by some sort of frame that ran up from the posts right up to the ceiling, with beautiful carvings in the wood all the way and on the headboard and base board. Again the carpet was thick and in this room a deep red colour she didn't know the name of. The window was massive and was draped on either side by thick velvet curtains of the same colour as the carpet, but most wondrous of all to her eyes was the sight of the floor to ceiling mirror that occupied half of one of the walls of the room. She actually gasped when she saw this.

"The bath is in through there" the maid said pointing, "It's already filled. There are towels and soaps for you to use in there as well... and some bedclothes too."

"Thank you" Kate said for a lack of being able to say anything else.

"I am to go get you something to wear and when you come out from the bath you are to use this bed to sleep until lunch. I'll come and get you at that time"

"Ok" Kate said trying to take it all in.

"And you are not to leave these two rooms until I come and get you ok? We can't have just anyone wandering the halls here"

"Yes, ok"

As you can imagine more wonders awaited Kate when she went into the bathroom but we needn't go into that here. She sank into the hot water of the bath and sank her head beneath the surface. No one else had used this water. She was in fresh clean hot water and she loved the feel of it against her body. She watched as her skin grew pink from the heat and she washed with the soaps that had been left out for her. She ran her frothy fingers through her hair and cleansed it as many times as she could without getting cramp in her hand and then finally she got out and dried herself with towels she would kill a person to be able to use all of the time.

She put on the bedclothes and she came back into the bedroom and looked at herself in the mirror. She was so excited at what she saw. She had never looked so fresh in her life and she was could smell the beautiful aromas of the soaps on her skin and in her hair. She looked around and seeing that there was no one who could see her she ran and jumped onto the bed in excitement.

She sank into it and it felt great and so comfortable but oddly the first thing that came into her head was that this bed would terrible to make love in. You would sink in too much and you wouldn't be able to do anything that you needed to. She put the thought out of her mind, determined to live in the present and to feel the moment she was in. She cleared a little space for herself at one side of the bed and she wrapped a blanket around her and soon she could feel the warmth of her body and she drifted off to sleep.

She was awoken a few hours later by the same maid who had seen her in that morning.

"Come on, up you get, lunch is in fifteen minutes" Kate stretched out and then the feeling of the bed reminded her where she was. She sat bolt upright and hoped she had not done anything wrong.

"What do I have to do?" she asked the maid with pleading eyes

"Getting dressed would be a good start" the maid said.

When she had done this, putting on the new clothes that the maid had brought for her (they were nothing fancy just a little more expensive than the clothes she would have herself anyway)she was escorted back down the stairs and into one of the rooms she had passed this morning. She felt so fresh and her body wanted to stretch out and enjoy the spacious surroundings.

Mr Edwards was at a table in this dining room reading a large newspaper. He glanced up as she came in but he did not stand and nor did he say anything before looking back at his paper. Kate didn't know what to do and when she looked at the maid for advice the maid did not look at her but faced her master with an indifferent look on her face. After a time Edwards folded the paper and looked at them both.

"Thanks, that will be all" and at this the maid left the room without a word. "Sit down" he then said to Kate indicating a chair at the table.

"Thank you" she said and sat.

"I expect you are hungry" he said lifting lids of the silver dishes that were spread about the table "take what you like" Kate was stunned to see much at one meal, and only for two people. She again thanked him and took some meat that she did not recognise and put it on her plate. She looked at the cutlery and saw that the table had settings for eight people but that where she sat was a little different to the others. At all the other places there were numerous knives, forks and spoons of differing sizes but at hers there was a single knife, fork and spoon.

"It is just to make it less confusing for you dear" Edwards said obviously noticing what she was looking at which embarrassed her.

He stood up and took her plate and filled it with food from each of the steaming dishes and then placed it back in front of her. It was more food than she had ever seen on one plate in her life, equivalent to a week's dinners she would normally have.

"Now, you get started on that and I will get started with my questions" he said filling his own plate. She began to eat and the hot food was something else her senses had missed so much. She closed her eyes to the feeling and she could feel the nourishment already in her saliva.

"OK" she said.

"What happened the night that Olocher was brought in?" he asked and the mention of that name again caused her to open her eyes and she looked about the place as if Edwards had just addressed him and he was in the room.

"It was a horrible night" she said

"How so?"

"Well the weather for one thing, it was streaming down"

"I'm not too interested in the weather. What happened when he got to the prison?"

"They brought him in and took him straight up into the tower without any questions or anything like normal"

"Do they normally ask questions when they bring a prisoner in?"

"Yes Jimmy the...Mr. Brick normally asks a lot of questions and has the person searched before you get thrown in a cell"

"Jimmy the Prick?" Edwards smiled and again Kate blushed at her error. "You don't have to blush on my account, that idiot is no associate of mine. Go on what next?"

"Well it was a normal enough night then for a while, nothing was going on and then all of a sudden there was the noise of a woman screaming from up in the tower"

"A woman screaming?"

"Yeah, that's what it sounded like anyway and then there was animals outside"

"The pigs?"

"Yeah, only a few at first but then there were loads, hundreds maybe"

"Hundreds?"

"Well it was hard to tell from the dungeon but that's how it seemed"

"And then what?"

"Well they all started squealin' it was like they were being slaughtered and then some of them tried to break in through the gates"

"Break in?"

"Yes they were thumping against the gates, we could see them moving from the inside"

"Remarkable"

"Yeah it was, and then it just stopped all of a sudden just like it had begun"

"The woman screaming as well as the pigs squealing?"

"I think so"

"Then?"

"Then there was a big to do with the guards and they found out that he was dead up there"

"Olocher?"

"Yeah, and then the soldiers came and there were other people coming and going all night"

"Do you know who these people were?"

"No, I didn't know any of them"

"Where they in the military do you think?"

"I couldn't be sure but they weren't wearing any uniforms"

Edwards was silent for a little now and he seemed to muse deeply on what she had said.

"And the next morning was the riot outside the prison?"

"Yeah, the people who went to see him hung showed up just as the body was being taken away. They went crazy and attacked the soldiers and took the body"

"Do you know who took the body?"

"I could see them but I don't remember ever seeing their faces before"

"When the body was found was it brought back to the prison?"

"No"

"And when the body was being taken away did you actually see it"

"Well it was covered in a sheet"

"Were you able to tell for sure that it was Olocher?"

"Well no, but it must have been" Kate was confused as to what he was saying but he didn't dwell here.

"Tell me about the night that the first guard was killed"

"We were asleep over at the wall away from the window trying to keep warm" Kate said and the thought of this made he put another hot piece of potato in her mouth, "and then there was this noise outside and we could hear the guard crying out in agony" she felt the hot flush of tears come to her as she remembered the event.

"Could you see anything at all, a shadow even?"

"No nothing"

"And the noise you heard before the guard crying out, what was it?

"I don't know, it sounded like an animal"

"What animal did it sound like?"

"I don't know, they all sound the same to me really" she said stifling her tears.

"They brought this man into the prison?"

"Yes and then the doctor came"

"What did he say?"

"He said it looked like some animal had done it"

"Did he say what animal he thought it might have been?"

"I think he said it could have been a dog"

"And they took him away to the hospital where he died. Can you remember anything else about that event?

"No, it seemed to happen so fast"

"Ok, what about the second guard?"

"I saw it that night, I was awake"

"You saw it?" he sat forward now and studied her seriously.

"Yes, first I heard it growling outside"

"Growling? Like a dog?"

"Could have been a dogs growl"

"And you saw it?"

"Yes, but I was so afraid that there were tears in my eyes when it passed by the cell window" again her tears were falling.

"What was it?"

"I couldn't tell" she cried out feeling as though she had let someone down by not being able to say what it was.

"Relax it's ok, here have a drink" he said pouring her some of the wine he was drinking. She took a mouthful and she almost choked on the taste of it, much different that the 'wine' she was used to drinking at the brothel. She coughed and then regained her breath again embarrassed by her display. "Could it have been a man?" he asked her.

"No, it was big and black and I'm sure it was on four legs, oh and those teeth!" she had just remembered this and she thought it odd that she should have an image of those sharp fangs now and to not have perceived them at the time.

"The teeth?"

"Yes they were huge, much bigger than you would expect for even a creature of that size"

"Did they bring this man into the prison?" Kate looked at him as though he were stupid.

"There was nothing left of him to bring in"

"Nothing?"

"Well, they had his torn clothes and his halberd but that was all"

"Did the doctor come again?"

"No, there was nothing for him to examine" again she wondered why he was asking such silly questions.

"Did anything else happen that night?"

"No"

"Did you notice anything odd on any of the other nights that you were there, anyone passing by the windows late at night or any strange noises in the area?" She thought about this but nothing was coming to mind. She could just sense the stench of the place in her nostrils and she almost retched at the thought of it.

"No, nothing I can remember anyway"

"Ok" he said and he thought for a while about what she had said. Kate took this opportunity to continue eating and she took some more small sips of the wine which was much better than she had though after the first taste.

Finally he stood up and she looked up at him.

"I will have my driver drop you home or to the brothel or wherever you want to go in a little bit"

"Thank you"

"I just want you to do one more thing before you go" he said with an evil smile as his hands began to undo his trousers.

Chapter 12

Superstition and rumour combined make one of the most powerful and persuasive concoctions known to man. After the two killings at 'The Black Dog' people started to talk and assumptions and gossip were repeated as facts throughout the markets, coffee houses and taverns. What was said was fanciful and outrageous but on these dark cold evenings the words began to gain traction and the fears of the people were given solid form.

It was said that the two guards who had been killed, the second one completely devoured- his body never found, had been particularly cruel to Thomas Olocher on the night he was in that prison. It was said that he cursed them and swore revenge-(this information apparently came from one of the soldiers who had been placed in the prison on duty that night) and that now his spirit was back and roaming the streets at night meeting out revenge to those whom Olocher felt deserved it.

Someone remembered the pigs that made way for Olocher's cart to get to the prison gates and others still could recall that night when hundreds of pigs gathered outside the gates of the prison and squealed as he killed himself and how they tried to force their way through the gates. When rumour spread of the hoof like marks on the chest of the first guard to be killed it was thought that Olocher's demonic spirit had entered the body of some feral mutant pig breed and was now out to kill who it could. Others said his evil was ingested by the very pigs that feasted on his body when it was found by the soldiers.

Sightings began to be recorded of large unidentifiable animals darting in the shadows and through the dark alleyways at night. Women used the name of Olocher (they called the beast The Olocher which was then shortened in the Dublin way by usage to D'Olocher and then finally metamorphosed into The Dolocher) to scare their children to make them go to bed at night or to stop being bold.

It was said that the Dolocher was a huge black pig that could walk on its hind legs like a man when it wanted, it could climb walls and get in through doors and windows. It had the massive teeth of a wolf. It would lie asleep in some lair by day and set forth at night to sate its evil appetites.

Of course these rumours were rubbish but there was no stopping them for the week after the second guard was killed. The streets were noticeably quieter at night now, especially in the area of Cornmarket and those streets that adjoined it.

People would scoff at this as mindless superstition and say that it was clearly the work of a mad man, that there was no such thing as evil spirits inhabiting animal bodies and other such nonsense. But even these people felt the chill wind of fear of the Dolocher if they were ever unfortunate enough to be alone in the city after dark, even if only for a few moments. They too would see the great black pig in the shadows of the large buildings, they would hear his growling deep into black alleys further than their eyes could penetrate.

Mullins sat and listened to the talk around him in his favourite whiskey cabin in Cook Street. He had always been fascinated by the way simple phrases and drunken comments in these places suddenly became gossip and fact the very next night, in some cases the same night. He had watched a few nights in a row now as the stories gathered and changed and coagulated into this new narrative of 'The Dolocher.'

Cleaves came in and sat down beside him and Mullins could feel the cold from outside on him.

"Another glass" Mullins called to the bar and a woman brought one over put it in front of him. Mullins poured a big drink for Cleaves.

"Full house tonight" Cleaves said looking around and raising his glass to Mullins.

"It gets fuller as the colder nights come in" Mullins said "People's homes are not as warm as these places and the whiskey has its own warmth as well" he smiled, his own cheeks feeling the heat he had just spoken of.

"No sign of the Dolocher out there tonight" Cleaves joked, Mullins felt that Cleaves shared his own scepticism of the tall tales that were doing the rounds. A few angry eyes looked his way but no one said anything.

"Too cold out there for him" Mullins laughed.

They spoke for a while about customers and work they had done this last few days (Cleaves worked unloading the ships that came to Temple Bar every day and he often saw things that Mullins found fascinating, he also did early morning deliveries for businesses some mornings) as they made their way through another jug.

"Who is that ugly fellow who has been eyeballin' this way all night?" Mullins asked Cleaves later on.

"He's Lord Muc" Cleaves said not having to look as he had noticed him watching them as well.

"The leader of the Liberty Boys?"

"The very same"

"That explains the state of his face so"

"He's probably spent half his life bleeding at this stage"

"Why do you suppose he's been watching us tonight?"

"No idea" Cleaves said "and I won't be asking him to find out" he smiled before adding "You shouldn't either"

As they spoke Lord Muc stood up and went to leave the cabin; he was tall, almost six feet and his frame was thick with undefined muscles and he was covered in scars. His left ear was mangled as though some animal had been chewing on it and his nose was bent many times in both directions and covered with pock marks. As he got to the door he leaned over to Mullins and said,

"I'll come and see you sometime this week"

"For what?" Mullins asked but Lord Muc didn't answer and he went out the door. Mullins looked at Cleaves. "What do you suppose he wants?"

"Probably wants you to fix weapons for him, or maybe make new ones"

"Well he will be disappointed if he does"

"You should be careful with them Mullins, you've seen yourself I'm sure what they are capable of"

"Fuck them" Mullins said and at that moment he would relish the chance to pop Lord Muc one in his ugly grizzled face. When he had his first violent thought of the evening he knew that it was time to stop drinking and go home.

He leaned to the table and he poured the rest of his glass back into the jar.

"I'm off home" he said to Cleaves who he was sure already knew the drill when he saw Mullins fail to finish his drink.

"Be careful out there Mullins"

"I will be"

"And go straight home" he said with a mocking mothers tone. Mullins smiled at him and stood up. He was a little uneasy on his feet and he stumbled against the door frame. Cleaves laughed and Mullins joined him.

From his standing position he could see that it was raining outside now and heavy.

"Shit, it's pissing out" he said out loud.

"Here use this since you brought it" Cleaves said laughing and holding something out to him. Mullins looked at it and for a moment he didn't recognise it out of context, not in the place where it always was. It was his big black leather apron that he wore while he worked. He had run out of his smithy earlier that day to deliver a finished job to a gentleman he'd arranged to meet in Hell and he had come straight from there to the whiskey cabin with the cash he had been paid. He took the heavy garment from Cleaves and arranged it over his head as he stepped out into the night with not another word said.

The rain was freezing as it hit his body, driving down at an angle that rendered his apron almost useless except for keeping the top of his head dry. It slapped against his face and body and he instantly lost the inner whisky glow and he cursed the sky. He was tempted to turn back but the fact that he was already wet through now and the idea of his clothes hardening to dryness on him changed his mind and he hurried on towards home.

When he got to his door he fumbled to open it and he could see in the moonlight that there was red stains forming on the ground around his feet, he looked up but could see nothing and then he realised that it was rusted metal fragments running down from his encrusted apron and turning the groundwater that same rust red. He finally got inside and out of the cold.

Chapter 13

Mary finished her work at the tavern on Wards Hill just off New Market, early tonight as the custom was slow. The owner sent her home so as not to have to pay her for the full evening. She protested but she had no power and she was told to go for the night or go for good. She needed the money so she had to swallow this less well paid night. When she left it was raining very heavily and there was a vicious chill in the water driving down, and it was falling so heavily that it seemed that the drops were bouncing right back off the ground and she was getting as wet from below and she was from above.

She rushed homewards in this foul weather rather than try shelter in some door or archway. She had heard in the course of her work of the terrible rumours about the killings at the prison and as you would expect they affected her more deeply than they would anyone else. She didn't believe the rumours but she couldn't stop them from pervading her thoughts every evening as she made her way home alone along the sometimes eerily quiet streets. She was so scared some evenings that when she rounded a corner and found a pig in the street she would double back and take another street to get where she was going, and as there were hundreds of these dirty beasts all over the city this could happen a few times every evening and would cause her sometimes to have to run past one on the opposite side of the street having exhausted all the routes home she knew.

On this night there was no one about and even the pigs had the sense to find shelter where they could. The noise of the rain slapping on the ground was all she could hear and not even her own scurrying footsteps registered in her ears.

Once or twice she thought she saw someone ahead but when she looked up to see properly there was no one there. It was probably someone darting into one of the buildings to escape the weather. She continued on regardless.

She was still living with Sarah (this was a month and half after she had been let stay for one night!) in Hanbury Lane. The walk home only took her fifteen minutes, pigs depending, and she always felt she was just about there when she reached the junction of Ash Street and Engine Alley. She could see this now and she quickened her pace with the thought of the dryness inside Sarah's place, the fire that would be possibly still be going now- it was normally down to embers by the time Mary got in. She would poke and crush them to get the last heat from them normally and fell that loved warmth for a few seconds before going to bed. She felt a little warmer even thinking there would be a fire.

Then she saw something move by the side of the wall ahead of her. This time she did stop. The movement hadn't looked natural and she was alarmed by what it might be. She looked around to see if there was anyone else there who might be able to assist her should she need it but no one was there. A sheet of rain slapped against her causing her to shut her eyes for a moment, the tide of it clearly approaching her from across the road before it did. She looked again to where she had seen movement. There didn't seem to be anything there now but she had seen it at the corner of Croslick a small street that she would have to pass to get to her junction.

She crossed over to the other side of Ash Street and edged forward slowly still trying to see something. The closer she got the more fearful she became and the driving rain and the rush of bubbling water at the roadsides were all she could hear. She could feel the cold rough brick of the buildings at her wet back as she shunted along trying to make herself as quiet and invisible as she could.

She could see a little into Croslick now but there was still a part hidden by the angle of the corner where someone may be lurking. She took a deep breath; the sound of her heart beating was now audible to her inside her head and she stepped out into the crossroads with Garden Lane to her back and now she could see across Ash Street down the full length of Croslick.

There was nothing there! The relief almost brought her to her knees and the pace of her heart seemed to lessen as she became even more aware of the thumping in her chest.

She breathed deeply again to try to calm her shaking body; her jellied legs and light head.

She felt the crash of her forehead into the road before she felt the effect of the strike from behind or the tumult of her fall. She was dazed for a second and then she heard the animal noises that she had so feared and she felt the ripping of the flesh of her upper back and she heard her clothes tear along with it. She screamed and tried to turn but the creature had his weight on her now, her legs were pinned under it grinding against the hard ground and she could feel more strikes and she could see glints of light on the dripping wet teeth and they smashed around her, sometimes hitting her and sinking into her and sometimes missing and making horrible screeching noises on the cobbles; there seemed to be flashes of sparks as it crashed the cobbles. Each slash was more painful than the last and still she struggled on trying to wriggle free, her hands swinging as much as she could behind her at her assailant. She twisted and writhed and once caught sight of one wild eye that didn't meet hers but didn't seem to be focused on anything.

Just as suddenly as it started she felt the weight lift from her body and then was aware of some men shouting and the sound of running footsteps. She was face down and she felt so weak and like she was going to pass out but the pain was keeping her conscious and she moaned in agony and ran her hand over her back to where it hurt the most. She could feel thick ridges that she couldn't understand and the pain was unbelievable.

Someone was talking to her but she couldn't focus on what they were saying and then she felt a new excruciating pain as she was lifted from the ground and she let out a howling wail before falling out of waking.

Chapter 14

When news began to spread about the attack on Mary Sommers; the same Mary Sommers who had witnessed Thomas Olocher's crime, the same Mary Sommers who was instrumental in having him sentenced to death, many could not believe anything other than the rumours that abounded about his soul in the body of some beast looking for revenge. To many there could be no other explanation, all of those attacked so far had done something against Olocher, it couldn't be a coincidence. How could an attacker have singled her out of all the women in Dublin if not for the reason that she was targeted? And who else would target a girl just turned fifteen if not The Dolocher?

When the soldiers were asking around about the houses to see if anyone had seen anything, there began to be something that might possibly be a lead. Though streets away from the attack there had been a man seen, a large man, walking in the rain with some kind of heavy black garment over his head. He had been in the Cook street area and when this was followed up more people had seen this same man enter Ushers Court. When the people of that place were asked they had seen the man enter Dog and Duck Yard. Further questions yielded the name of Timothy Mullins as this same man and it was said it was his leather apron that he had over his head when he came home that night. It was said that he was as drunk as a lord as he got to his door.

Was it usual for him to carry his apron about with him when he went drinking? The soldiers asked his neighbours. No was their answer and this led them to their supposition that this was the black beast people had spoken of as The Dolocher. Someone had even noticed that when he got home that night there was blood running from his apron when he got to the door. The time of his arrival home was within ten minutes of the attack on Mary Sommers.

This was evidence enough to question Mullins about his whereabouts that evening. The officer stepped into Mullins home as his soldiers waited outside. Mullins knew that the soldiers had spoken to many people and he was ready to answer all the same questions they had but he was not expecting the blunt question that came from the officer.

"Did you attack a woman last night?"

Mullins was stunned, his eyes opened wide with disbelief.

"No" he stammered still reeling with the shock of the accusation.

"You came home last night with your apron over your head?" the officer said.

"Yeah, it was raining"

"Was there blood on this apron?"

"No" he was confused to this question, why would he think there was blood on it?

"Is this the apron?" the officer asked placing his hand on a leather apron on the table

"Yes"

The officer picked it up and examined it.

"What is all this red stuff on it?" he asked and showed it to Mullins. Before he could see it properly he was nervous, the connection between the question of blood, an attack on a woman and now red stains on his apron tied together in his mind and he could feel guilt rising that he knew had place to.

"That's just rust residue, I'm a blacksmith and metal gets on the apron the whole time. That's what it's for" He was relieved when he saw the stains.

"Is any of it blood?"

"No, blood is not that colour, this is more orange"

"How do you know what colour blood is?" the officer asked and again Mullins was surprised by his questions.

"I have bled before" he answered hoping not to sound insolent.

"Of course" the officer said and he put the apron down on the table. "Where were you last night?"

"I was in the whisky cab on Cook Street"

"The what?"

"The whisky cabin on Cook Street"

"Oh 'Cabin'" the officer had been making some point here but it was lost on Mullins. "What time did you leave?"

"About eleven I think"

"You think?"

"Yes, I was a little drunk" Mullins was embarrassed to say this but thought he should tell the truth.

"Drunk enough to attack a woman and then forget about it?"

"No never!" Mullins cried out. "You can ask the owner he will tell you I left at that time. I came straight home. It's only a few minutes from door to door"

"Why did you have your apron with you last night?"

"I was in a rush to deliver a piece to a customer in Hell and I still had it on as I ran out of the store, otherwise I was going to be late and I mightn't have got paid"

"You didn't think to bring it home or back to the store before you went drinking?" the officer asked and Mullins knew it was purely to embarrass him.

"No" he said looking at the ground. He was sure this was what the officer wanted to see.

"Did you see anyone on your way home?"

"Not a soul"

"It was raining heavily" the officer said and Mullins nodded. "Well that will do for now but you may be questioned again when I file my report"

"Ok" Mullins answered.

"Good day" the officer said and he left the building. Mullins was at the door and he saw the officer poke his foot at the rust stains on the ground just outside.

"That's not the same colour as blood" the officer smiled to him and he marched off followed by his troops.

Mullins went back inside and he sat down at the big table. He looked at the rust stains on the apron, the rain had really brought them out worse than even before. The apron was rigid from being so wet and its weight much more than before. He picked at some of the deep orange flecks of dried residue and he remembered the red liquid running off it onto the ground at his door last night, an image he had not remembered until just now. The lantern lights had given it a strange hue, changed the natural orange to a watery dull red, a flowing dull red. He put it down and went to his window and looked out. There were not many people around and who was there were long standing neighbours.

How could anyone think him capable of hurting a woman? Some of these very neighbours must have thought he had done it to tell the soldiers that there was blood running from his apron when he got home. It was sickening a thought that there was that much distrust in a small street like this, with all of them in the same boat, doing nothing other than trying to put food on the table from day to day. Who could think he could attack a woman? He had a little temper when drunk and he'd had his fair share of fights with sailors or other men in the taverns and whiskey cabins but that was no different to anyone else who went there. Who?

Chapter 15

Mullins was seeing a customer out when Lord Muc came from across the road. He had been out there for about an hour and he had been watching Mullins all the time. Mullins had looked back a few times but there was no change in the face of the gang leader.

"What are you looking for?" Mullins said when he finally came over and entered the blacksmiths, there was an edge to his tone that he hadn't fully intended but didn't altogether regret either; it was more than likely he was going to be delivering bad news to this man anyway so why be pleasant at the outset?

"We need you" Muc said

"For what?" Mullins asked, he wasn't sure what he was being asked for.

"To join"

"To join!" Mullins laughed

"Yeah, there is another battle coming and I think with you on our side we can finish those Ormonde pricks off for good"

"What difference to your little 'army' do you think I'd make?" Mullins mocked him, he had been annoyed by Muc's usage of the term battle to describe the street fights the Liberty Boys and the Ormonde Boys engaged in periodically. There was nothing of the honour of battle involved in these vicious tit for tat brawls.

"I saw you fight one night a few weeks ago on Cook Street. You were out of your head drunk but you still managed to take out four guys all about the same size as yourself" Muc said with a sneer that may have been intended as a camaradic smile.

"Fighting in taverns and mindless street thuggery are two different things. People go to taverns just to have fights sometimes, to get the anger out of them, to rid them of poisons" Mullins said and wondered was he describing himself or the people he fought with.

"Fighting is fighting and you can get rid of all the poison you want in one of our fights" Muc said excited now, a flick of life animating his dark eyes as he spoke of his passion.

Mullins looked at him and he could almost sense something sexual in the chemistry talking about fighting had aroused in his visitor. This was a man who didn't rid himself of anything by fighting but who took something on by doing it. Did he think it was some great strength giver or elixir?

"I'm not interested" Mullins said and he turned back to his forge.

"That might not be a wise choice" Muc said.

Mullins turned to face him.

"Is that supposed to be a threat?" he spread his shoulders as wide as he could and stepped closer to Muc who gave a good four inches on the blacksmith. Muc didn't seem fazed at all and though he didn't want to look away from his eyes Mullins could sense that his fists were balled and ready to be used.

"Not at all. I just don't think you are making the right decision" Mullins didn't respond this time. "You know the way you feel when you fight? Well this is a hundred times more intense and what's more is the man you are fighting has set out to fight and so accepts anything that comes his way" Muc's eyes were wild now and he was clearly remembering something he had done before. "You can kill and there is no victim, only a willing combatant who would do the same to you if he could"

There was something almost hypnotic in his eyes and the way he spoke and Mullins was sure that many a lost and hungry man had been roped into this gang with that very same speech, but he was still not interested.

"I fight to blow off steam the odd time not because I'm violent. I have no desire to kill or be killed by anyone"

"I should have known" Muc said "you only like killing women"

"If you ever say anything like that to me again it will be you I'll be killing!" Mullins shouted at him but Lord Muc had already turned his back and was walking out and Mullins could hear him chuckle at the threat as he waved a dismissive hand in the air as he passed under the door frame.

Mullins was angry now as he knew that it wasn't just his neighbours who thought him capable of attacking a women but the rumour had spread all over the Liberties by now and there would be no shortage of people who would be willing to believe it. He just couldn't believe that people could think this of him, who did they think he was if not the blacksmith who for years has done all they have asked of him?

For the rest of that day he worked hard and was gruff with any customer who happened to come in. He didn't want to see anyone and he was blaming them all for how he was feeling. Faces of neighbours and people he saw everyday kept coming to mind and he could feel their sneer as they looked down on him and called him killer behind his back. He could feel a swell of violence come up in him and he wished that Lord Muc would come back now and try to goad him some more so that he could vent his rage on that ugly smarmy face.

He got more angry as he knew that Lord Muc would only be delighted to know that he had caused such a reaction in him; a reaction that he would see as proof that Mullins was who Muc said he was and a step closer to unleashing that same poison he had spoken of. He wondered did Lord Muc even want him in the gang or did he just want to see him erupt in an orgy of violence that would reverberate and mix with the undertones of pain and suffering that spread its dark flow over this city. Could he be what people thought even when he felt so different to that view? Was he violence? Was Dublin violence? There is a killer or wild animal on the loose and yet there is still the everyday violence of life to contend with. Did the Dolocher grow out of this same city of violence?

Chapter 16

Alderman James was sitting at the same table Kate had lunched at in the dining room at Mr. Edwards's house. They had just enjoyed a large dinner and Edwards was drinking brandy and James coffee.

"Do you lot ever stop drinking alcohol?" James smiled at him.

"Not if we can help it" Edwards laughed back, "The world can be a dull place without it"

"You've heard I'm sure by now of the Sommers girl being attacked?" James asked knowing full well that Edwards did and probably knew more than he did about it.

"Indeed" Edwards replied quaffing his drink, "I was in the vicinity when it occurred"

"You saw it?" James asked sitting forward and Edwards smiled,

"No, no, I was on Francis Street in one of our club houses when it happened"

"You heard it then?"

"No, when you are at a Hellfire gathering you don't hear anything that goes on outside I can assure you" he laughed.

"Well, anyway, you are aware no doubt of this ridiculous rumour in the lower classes about the soul of Thomas Olocher being responsible for the attacks?"

"I have and to be fair to them you can see why a person with no education would believe such a thing"

"Yes I suppose" James agreed, "Now with this attack on the witness who sent him down it is all but gospel truth over in the Liberties and Hell and spreading outside those areas as well"

"I can imagine"

"We have been getting reports of sightings of all kinds of animals all over the place in the last few days" James said scornfully "There was even a report of a huge black elephant!"

"How do you think all this fear will manifest itself?" Edwards asked seriously when he stopped chuckling about the elephant.

"I don't know but I have been thinking about what you said the other night about it being an animal come in on a ship"

"That was just idle talk"

"Yes I know but idle talk is how gossip starts. I have extra patrols near the docks but I have asked them to be as discreet as possible"

"You think if that rumour starts there will be a riot against the ships?"

"I do"

"Well, you and I both know that there will be an explosion of some kind when the people get scared enough but it is often difficult to guess in what form that will take"

James thought about this as he sipped more of the thick bitter coffee. He was doing what he could to redeem his name and this riot that he could feel coming was going to have to be put down somehow and that would probably mean the army again and he may be forced into the same position as before, only this time it will be the scared and not the angry who were rioting and they were a different kettle of fish altogether. He had to catch whoever was responsible as soon as possible.

"What do you think of this blacksmith?" James asked and as expected Edwards knew who he was talking about.

"Timothy Mullins" he said "I don't see it. I went to his house and saw the red at his door, clearly rust and his story about a delivery to a client in Hell is true as well, I have checked that out. He left the pub and got home in what seems to be a five minute window which would be about right for the walk he had to do. I actually have my own suspicions about who it might have been"

James perked up at this, his hopes raised at once by this man who seemed always to know everything before he did.

"Who?"

"In the course of my questioning I came across another piece of information which I also followed up"

"What was it?"

"Someone left the cabin just before the blacksmith and the direction they went was not the direction home for this person"

"Who?"

"Someone you know well who has a propensity for violence" Edwards hinted, James could see he was enjoying this.

For a moment James thought he meant a gentleman who was liberal with his fists after a few drinks and he racked his brain trying to think who it might be but then he realised that no one he knew would frequent such a place as a whiskey cabin on Cook Street. It must be a criminal who was well known to him.

"There are many criminals well known to me who could have been there that night"

"Yes but this one fits very well with the crimes committed"

"Tell me man!"

"Lord Muc" Edwards smiled

"The Liberty Boys leader?" It seemed unlikely. Lord Muc loved violence but he liked it in the pitched sense on open ground and with his gang around him. He couldn't see him skulking around at night and attacking with stealth; he was too boisterous for that.

"That's him yes" Edwards answered. "He left the cabin about ten minutes before Mullins. Lord Muc lives in Schoolhouse Lane which would mean that he would turn left when he left the cabin on Cook Street but I have it on good authority that he turned right and then went up New Row"

"Good authority?"

"One of our lads was on the way to the meet on Francis Street and saw him"

"And who was this?"

"He is above suspicion Alderman and as such there is no need to use his name"

"Lord Muc has not been questioned as far as I know" James said.

"He fits the bill in a couple of ways I think. He is violent, sneaky, he was drunk at the time and walking the streets in terrible weather. Do you know what Muc is the Irish for by the way?"

"No"

"Pig" Edwards smiled.

"You don't say!" James said.

"Yes, it seems crude but apparently he has worked with pigs in the past and that is where he got the moniker he goes by. He would probably have access to pig body parts and hides and he could be using them as a disguise to deflect the rumours to the gossip about Olocher" Edwards said almost seeming to muse out loud.

"I'll have someone talk to him" James said.

"It is only a slight suspicion Alderman and one which I don't believe is true; in fact I would be quite disappointed if it were true"

"Then why tell me?" James said, annoyed now by the playful attitude Edwards was always adopting.

"It could be right, the circumstantial evidence is all there and even if it is not true it will start new rumours"

"What good is that?"

"With this blacksmith and now Lord Muc being questioned seriously about these crimes the rumour mill will steer away from wild horror stories of demon pigs and focus on evil men with evil intent; something that the general populace is not all that afraid of" Edwards smiled

"And when they are not afraid anymore the chances of a riot diminish accordingly?"

"Exactly Alderman. This is what you call a win win situation"

James sat back in his chair and he wondered if there was ever anything in Edwards' life that wasn't a win for him. He didn't like the network this man had for getting information and he was always keeping the names of his Hellfire Club friends out of affairs. They were a wild lot and he would not have been all that surprised to find them responsible for a lot more than they got credit for.

The riot had to be avoided at all costs or else people were going to die. He was going to have to order that people die. His mind jumped from this to Lord Muc and he thought of the famous elephant dissection in Temple Bar over a hundred years ago. Not many of the lower classes would know anything about that but he could only imagine what would happen if people started to believe there was a killer animal of that size on the prowl at night.

This riot had to be avoided at all costs. He would have to go to the streets himself and catch this killer. That was the only was he could be both sure that it was done and sure that he could perhaps redeem himself in the eyes of those people he so sought.

Chapter 17

Mullins stood at the door of the blacksmith waiting. He had just finished a job for a customer and he was awaiting a delivery of some odds and ends that some gentleman was looking to have spruced up and straightened out. As he waited he took in the cool air away from the furnace heat inside. His eyes fell on a young potato seller and he knew that he had seen her before. There was something about her that was different now that drew his eye and as he looked he saw that she was limping badly and then he could just make out the scars that adorned her face now. She was the young girl who had been attacked and had survived it. He felt sorry for her as he remembered once buying two potatoes from her and how nice she had seemed to him then. She was only a child, how could anyone do anything like that too her?

As he watched her sell he noticed another woman come up behind her. This was an older girl and there was something altogether more womanly about the way she held herself as she waited for the seller to complete her transaction. She was brown haired and had beautiful eyes and he knew he had seen her before too and he remembered now where. She was a street walker and he was used to seeing her under the cover of darkness as he might pass her in the street or see her through the window of a tavern as he looked outside.

Seeing her in daylight seemed to change her in way that changed everything about her. Instead of seeing her as a profession he saw her as a woman, the same as any other he might see in the course of trading hours. She glanced at him quickly before starting to talk to the girl. They were laughing about something and they seemed to be friends.

A boy arrived with the things from the gentleman, a lot of old rubbish at first glance. As Mullins brought it in he allowed himself one more glance at the woman before setting about his work. He found his glance replied and there was a look in her eyes as though she were saying something to him but he had no experience of the looks of women and he would never be able to fathom it, she left to go about her business and he set to work now with an odd sense of melancholy sitting over him.

Some more work came in and by the time he finished that evening it was long dark outside. His shoulders ached and he was sweating from the work and the heat all day. He could smell the stale odour form his own body and it mixed with the damp leather of his apron and was very strong.

The air outside was welcome at first but even as he locked up the shop he began to feel the chill rip through his skin and get into his very bones. He would have to get home or into a crowded tavern as soon as possible if he wanted to avoid catching a chill. Either way he could go in the same direction and he started walking deciding to choose on his way what to do. There were still many people about the streets coming and going and some of the other traders were still opened. He looked into milliners, tobacconists and cloth shops as he made his way home. As he passed the Chocolate House, the only one he knew of, the smell was so intoxicating he was tempted to go in and have one, but nice smell or no he knew that it was massively expensive and not something he could afford to waste any money on.

When he was almost at Bridge Street he came face to face with the woman from earlier. He stepped out of her way and smiled with an awkward face that he felt sure would be seen by her as a strange grimace. She smiled at him and stopped instead of passing.

"Hello" she said

"Good evening" he said in return. She looked him over and stood there still with a brazen face on her. He didn't know what to say to her. Was she touting him? He hadn't used a prostitute before and wouldn't have a clue as to how to go about it.

"Are you married?" she asked

"No" he said "Who'd have a mug like this" he managed attempting a joke.

"There's much more to a good man than his face" she smirked. He shuffled from foot to foot and he was aware of how he smelled again that moment.

"You look cold, you better get home and warm yourself" she said and now he felt relief that this ordeal was almost over and yet he longed for it to go on, for them to talk some.

"Working in the heat all day can make the cold seem worse than it really is when you first come out of the smithery" he smiled (grimaced?)

"Get yourself in front of a fire. Goodbye for now" she said cheerily and went off as he said goodbye himself. He watched her as she walked away.

That night he found he couldn't stop thinking about her. He lit a fire and changed his clothes and made some hot soup all in an effort to heat himself but all the while he was thinking about getting back out that night and the possibility of running into her again. He didn't even know her name and he had no idea how he would ever approach her. He saw her eyes in his mind and then he saw them drop as into sadness and he felt that was all she would be if she were to ever be with him- sad. What did he have to offer? A small home and a generally steady income; that was a lot more than a lot of people could say. His face was a mess of bumps and his cheek was badly scarred but he was honest and hardworking, did those things count for anything with women?

He couldn't help but think of them as a family in this small home with a child or two; the image popped in there as though it had always been in his mind to settle down with this woman. Had he always wanted a family? His own parents hadn't been much to base life on. Could he marry someone who did what she did for a living? Would he ever get past that? Would she ever get past that?

And then he knew that the fact that it was an issue at all, which he hadn't realised up to this very moment, meant that he would never get past it. How could he be with a woman when almost any man they might meet in street might have shared a bed with her? He couldn't and it was bound to happen, someone he knew right now could have already been with her- could be with her right now! He was getting angry now and it he felt his rage towards her for tempting him at all; if that was what she was doing? But then maybe she was just looking for a new customer and he fit the bill nicely with his job and nice quiet place to have her in. That must have been it. She just wanted to use him for what he had. Had she not heard that his neighbours thought he was the Dolocher?

The family drifted from memory like paper tossed into the fire and it floated momentarily before blackening and falling apart to be sucked up into the chimney.

Chapter 18

The next person to be attacked in Dublin was not so fortunate as Mary Sommers had been. She was a young prostitute and was found on Kennedy Road with her neck savaged and wads of flesh missing from her cheeks and arms. She had massive bruising and was cut and scratched all over, her clothes torn to pieces.

She was found by a butcher and his son who were going to open their shop early for the busy docking day ahead in Temple Bar. Her name was Jill and she was well known in the local area as well meaning and kind. It was a horrible thing for those two to come across that freezing morning.

The rumour mill went into convulsions, doing cartwheels and somersaults to link this girl to Olocher. Olocher had been a customer of hers many times some said; others said she was one of the women he had beaten before and he had come back to finish the job. Still more said that she had been a secret witness at the trial and had also been responsible for Thomas Olocher going to jail just the same as Mary Sommers.

Though none of these things were true they all gained traction in different quarters. The one thing that was true was she had been killed in a savage manner, with teeth marks and hoof marks on her body that fit with the other attacks by The Dolocher.

Kate knew her and had worked some nights alongside her. They were not close at all but they were friendly. Kate was terribly upset when she heard what had happened, especially the lurid version of her physical state when found, but she quickly came to realise that she was so upset at the thought that it could just have easily been her. Street walkers had by definition to walk the streets and often times they were alone. The weekend nights she worked in the brothel and she felt safe there but the rest of the week she relied on casual trade for survival. She had to walk the streets if she wanted to eat.

She could try her luck during the day but it was hard to get any customers during the day. Hers was a profession that required the cover of darkness and the evenings of men spent in taverns. There were some of course who use her during the day here and there but it was harder to find a place to work and the chances of being caught in the act multiplied a hundredfold.

Kate left her home at about eleven and went to the market for food. She bought a few carrots and parsnips but thought better of buying anything more. She had very little money but she always liked to have something to her name.

As she was buying her vegetables she spoke to the seller. This is where she heard about the latest attack. At this point she didn't know who the victim was but she wondered if she might know them.

"A girl who lives with me was attacked by The Dolocher just last week" the seller said.

"Really! Mary Sommers?" Kate said.

"Yes, a friend of her aunt who Thomas Olocher killed lives with us and she brought her in"

"How is she?"

"Better but she is very scared now of everything, especially after dark"

"You can understand that"

"She'll have some scars to show for it but she'll be alright in the long run"

"There'll be a lot afraid to leave their doors in the evenings now"

"I know I won't be going anywhere myself"

"Does Mary Sommers remember anything more about her attacker?"

"No, I don't think so. It happened to her so fast she said, and she gets upset when she talks about it. She just says it was wild whatever it was and like nothing she had ever seen before" Kate shuddered at the thought of this creature pouncing on her.

As she looked over the food arrayed all around her and felt the lightness of her purse she thought to ask the seller,

"Do you know anyone decent looking to share a room?"

"Things tight?"

"Always" Kate smiled.

"I'll keep my ear out for you"

"Thanks"

Kate was turning to leave when the seller called her back, she handed her a few mouldy looking carrots and said,

"Here, they don't look like much but there will be some decent orange in there once you cut away the outside"

"Thank you" Kate said taking them

"Don't worry about it, no one was going to buy those ones today" and she laughed a loud cackle that seemed to disappear into the market noises all around them.

As she looked to follow this sound with her eyes Kate noticed the new ships queued along the Liffey. It was going to be busy for her trade for the next few nights, at least that was something to be thankful for. She decided she would go to the brothel and she if she could work for a day or two in the hope of staying off the streets.

She walked straight to the brothel in Hell and went to the lady of the house, Melanie (a French madam who had been much sought after by the gentlemen of the upper classes when she first arrived almost twenty years ago- this was how she had bought the large house in the first place) and asked to work there that night telling her about the amount of ships in the Liffey waiting to unload.

"You are a good girl for me and popular with some of my finest clients but I am full until the weekend dearie" Melanie said with a warm smile on her face. Kate was dismayed and it must have shown on her face. " Call in if you want and if any of the girls are unwell or not here I will put you first on the list for replacement?"

"Thank you Mel" Kate said and she smiled at the lady; the girls were always getting sick or not able to work because a client had beaten them up or some other disaster had happened. She was sure to get some work here over the next few days and that would lessen her need to be on the streets.

"For future reference Katie" Melanie said as she was leaving "I have the logs from the docks at all times. I am always well aware as to how many ships are coming and going"

That night she called in but there was nothing for her. She was surprised that everyone had shown up and she left and wondered what to do. She didn't want to prowl the alleyways and streets of the Liberties tonight nor did she fancy a walk anywhere near Francis Street or up at New Market. She went down to Temple Bar to see what she could get.

On cold nights like these the profession she had really got on top of her and depressed her. When she was in a bed at the brothel sleeping with men for money it didn't seem all that bad but when all she was doing was trudging around in the rain and sucking sailors for the price of her next bowl of soup she could cry at her existence.

The docks were busy and she was taken on board a couple of ships for a few minutes at a time but she wasn't earning much. It seemed even worse to her now that she had seen first-hand the opulence that people like Mr Edwards lived in. She remembered the bed and the bathroom and the carpet beneath her feet. At times she fantasised about a gentleman taking her in. She was not so naive that she ever thought any would ever marry her but she dreamt of just living in the same house as one of them and doing what they wanted of her when required.

When the dock quietened down somewhat she began to be afraid of the creaking of the ropes that moored the ships and the billowing in the loosely wrapped sails when a nasty wind whipped up. Each time the sound would frighten her; it was actually a very loud sound when there wasn't much for it to compete with. Her nerves were getting the better of her and her customer base was shrinking and so she went home in the hope that tomorrow would be a better day.

She went to the market the following day again, not to buy anything this time but just to pass the time. She had been home early and had gone to bed much earlier than before and so she was bored by mid-morning which was when she usually slept until.

As she browsed the stalls at the market she heard the vegetable seller from the day before call her over.

"Are you still interested in having someone share your room?"

"Yes"

"The very girl I told you about yesterday is looking to move out of our place. She says there are too many of us now"

"Mary Sommers!" Kate said in surprise

"Well not exactly, Sarah is who I was talking about. She was a friend of Mary's aunt who was killed"

"Oh"

"But to be honest I'd say she will want to take Mary with her"

Kate thought about this for a moment. She had heard such terrible things about 'The Dolocher' and she didn't want to invite that beast to her doorstep but she was desperate now. Thin soups were all she was eating lately and she was making less and less at work with all the country girls who were flocking to the city. She reasoned with herself that this monster was attacking people at night in dark streets and not going into houses. If he wanted Mary Sommers he could have her, Kate just wouldn't go anywhere outside the house with her. There was no need for roommates to be friends. All Kate really wanted was the money she would get from these two new housemates.

"Well, I need all the money I can get" Kate said and thus a few days later Sarah and Mary moved in to her small room on the second floor of a building on Skippers Lane.

Chapter 19

The candles in the tavern were lit in patterns leaving gaps so that the collected light remained low. They had been reignited with flames from the bonfire on the corner that blazed in honour of the great festival of Halloween. It was very subdued on this year's streets; people felt that it was in bad taste to dress up as animals when the Dolocher was roaming the streets and others were too frightened to go out after dark for that same reason. Some did dress up and go about the night as they did every year; some of the students from Trinity College even dressed as what they considered the Dolocher would look like. In this tavern in the Liberties there was no one so garish and the men that gathered there drank and spoke in low voices out of respect for the dead.

"Tell us one about Halloween Cleaves" someone said and all eyes went to the table he, Mullins and another tradesman sat at. When he didn't protest people began to come over, the scratch of wooden chairs on the floor as they all gathered around.

Mullins looked at Cleaves and watched him as he looked about the crowd trying to create the atmosphere that he wanted before starting. Mullins had seen this many times before over the years. Silence grew and Cleaves let it fester before he said anything. Mullins could feel his own apprehension growing even though he knew what was probably coming such was the dark silence that set in the room.

"Samhain is what the ancient Celts called this special holiday where the dead walked among the living" Cleaves began seriously. "The druids would be able to tell people's fortunes better on this night than on any other. The people would dress up using animal heads and hides to blend in with the walking dead amongst them" Mullins was sure he was not alone now in thinking of the Dolocher when he said this.

The room was quiet now and the candle flickers showed the dappled shadows of these wild dead and alive creatures on the lighted walls. Mullins took a deep drink as he imagined the scenes all those years ago. "The bonfires were lit and houses were kept in darkness and then lit from the flames of the bonfires for luck. Animal sacrifices, and it is said human sacrifices, were often offered up to appease the gods and the dead" No one was saying anything but it could be felt in the room that though the people respected the festival of Halloween they were not too interested in its history. What they had wanted from Cleaves was a ghost story set around Halloween and Cleaves must have felt it too.

"Enough of the history lesson lads!" he said cheerfully, "Time for a little tale I think?" he looked about the now smiling and animated faces that lit up at the prospect. "This one happened a long time ago in central Europe" he told them and then he told this tale,

"Once in the centre of Europe there was an old abandoned castle near a small town. This castle had been abandoned for a very long time and it was said that the noble family who once inhabited it were all murdered within its walls and the murderer was never found out or brought to justice. This happened so long ago that no one then living in the town had been alive at the time and they had heard the story passed down from parents and grandparents over the decades. People would always say that the castle was haunted by the ghosts of the dead and there were numerous sightings of ghostly figures walking about the grounds. Everyone was afraid of the place and no one had been inside its walls for as many, many years.

"One day a knight showed up on horseback and he made no secret of his arrival. He challenged any man to any task to prove his worth and proclaimed his fearlessness. He told tales and stories of his adventures and his bravery to everyone in town. The people grew quickly tired of his bravado and antics however and men stopped answering his call. He soon heard about the castle and he vowed to go into it and walk to the top of the stairs and plant a red spike to prove he had been up there.

"This was enough to get the attention of the people again and they all gathered in an area close enough to be able to see the entrance when the knight went in. They were all terrified that they would hear his terrible screams but the draw of curiosity was simply too strong for them to stay away.

"On his way to the castle the knight bowed and smiled to the people as he passed but he began to notice their fearful faces and it seeped into his brain that maybe there was something to be afraid of in that castle. He did his best not to show his fear and he could not refuse to do the task after all his boasting now. He dismounted his horse that refused to go nearer the castle and he waved once more to the people before he went in through the heavy wooden door which was ajar and warped from damp and wind over the years.

"Inside he could hear the echoes of water drips from all parts of the castle. It was cold inside and webs covered the walls like wool tapestries in a lot of places. Some light came in from damage in the ceiling high above him but it threw deeper gloom to where it did not light up. The air smelled of thick mould. He took the spike and mallet from his cloak and he began to walk up the stone steps which had been worn smooth by the wind over the years, or was it from the soft tripping's of ghostly footsteps? As he did he grew more afraid and he was convinced he could hear someone moving around but where the sound came from he could not tell. Half way up he heard his horse neigh and run from outside and the sound rattled around the hall and stairway and had him plunge his back to the wall and his hands rise to defend himself. His heart thundered and he glanced back down from where he had come. He was more than halfway up the stairs now but he was becoming more and more sure that there was something up there moving around the landings waiting for him. He couldn't go back down without completing his task. He went on one step at a time until he could lean forward and see around the corners at the stop of the stairs. He heard the noise that had been so scary to him and he looked and saw that it was a large tapestry on the wall moving and scraping in the wind and he let out a sigh of relief, glancing the other way just to be sure that there was nothing there either. He sat down in relief and took a few deep breaths and like your or I when we have ourselves a little scare we have a little chuckle at our own folly afterwards. He took his spike and placed it firmly at the centre of the top step of the stairs and he struck it three times heavily with his mallet. The noise was deafening with the ringing of the metal on stone and the spike stuck into the step. He was sure that everyone outside would have been able to hear the strikes. As he stood up to walk back down the stairs he heard the noise of movement again and then in terror he felt something grab hold of his cloak as he tried to walk away. He died of fright without ever turning to see what it was.

"When he was in there a long time the men of the town decided that they would go in as one to see what was going on. After a long time of going to the door and running away in fear they finally went in and they found the knight frozen in terror as though he was in flight from the top of the stairs but when they got to him they saw his cloak spread out behind him and nailed with the red spike to the top step of the stone stairs."

The faces around the table grew into large smiles and men looked at one another for reactions to the story, nodding their approval and winking at Cleaves, some telling how good that one was and asking for a drink for him. Mullins had not heard that story himself before and he thought it was a good one. He wondered where Cleaves constantly heard about all these things and how he remembered them all so well; he had asked before but Cleaves just winked and tapped his nose and wouldn't tell him.

Happy with what they had received some of the men were asking for more but Cleaves waved them away in his amicable way and promised more on another day. The group around the tables shuffled back to the other reaches of the tavern and soon the place was as it would be on any other night of the week. Outside in the night fires burned all over the city and candles indoors were low; the city was darkest just outside the light and fear lurked behind the festivities of all.

Chapter 20

Alderman James arrived at the 'Black Dog' to the vociferous throng of people in the streets surrounding the entrance. They were shouting things like "Bring him out!" And "Just hang him now!" and it had all the hallmarks of the riot he had so feared these last weeks. Before even leaving his carriage he called an officer over and ordered him to get more soldiers to police the streets adjacent to the prison.

As he stepped down from his carriage he saw Edwards standing across the street, leaning against a building and watching him. As they made eye contact Edwards shook his head from side to side with pursed lips. James wasn't sure what he meant but he had the terrible feeling that Edwards was saying that the man James had come to see, the man who had been caught in the act of trying to kill a woman by tearing at her flesh with meat hooks was not the elusive 'Dolocher' everyone here wanted him to be. The woman had since died of her injuries.

This did not bode well. The crowd here was clearly seeking a release from their nightly terrors and he could see now why sometimes it was better to have summary justice and have an innocent man condemned for the sake of larger public unrest and paranoia erupting as a result of the public's fears. If he came out here and told this baying crowd that they had not in fact captured the 'Dolocher' there would be uproar and the consequences would be unpredictable.

He didn't make any reaction to Edwards's grave nodding and he ignored the people who jostled about him and asked him for the hangman's rope as he made his way inside the soldiers cordon at the gates and then into the prison.

When he got inside he was met by the gaoler Brick who straight away began badgering him about the man held there.

"You have to get him out of here Alderman James! This is a debtor's prison; the last time we had someone in here for murder there was uproar and there was riots in the street outside. This place has not been the same since then!"

"Just bring me to him and we will get this all sorted as soon as we can"

"He needs to go to the barracks" Brick said but he started off up the stairs to where the new prisoner was under heavy guard. He was not going to let another man commit suicide in his prison.

When James came to the door he was surprised by the man he saw there in chains. It was a small thin emaciated man with a wild look in his eyes and a body that seemed ready to pounce at any time despite the upright standing position he was currently in. In his heart James already knew that Edwards was right but this man was still a killer none the less.

"What's your name" he asked the man.

"Mick Carolan" he answered in an almost sweet country brogue from somewhere in the west of Ireland but as to where, James couldn't place.

"Who was the woman you killed?" At this the man looked at the ground and seemed ashamed suddenly.

"I don't know"

"You don't know! Then why did you kill her?"

"She was making fun of me"

"About what?"

"She was disparaging about my manhood" and all the regret in the world seemed to be flooding into this man.

Every word he uttered seemed to tame that wildness that was in him and he grew more and contrite in appearance by the second. Most probably he had been roaring drunk when he did this and was sobering up fully only know and was aware of what he had done and for no good reason. James felt a slight kinship with this man in light of his own regrets for his acts committed in heat.

"Have you killed anyone else before?"

"No sir"

"Why were you carrying those meat hooks?"

"I carry them when I'm out at night, you know, because of the 'Dolocher.'" James didn't believe this, the man was not a good liar.

"You are in a lot of trouble for murder so I don't think you admitting to being in a gang is going to do you any more harm. Lying to me might however" James said firmly.

"Sorry sir. I am in a gang"

"Is there a fight coming up?" James thought he might as well gleam a little more information if he could.

"One is coming sir but I don't know when or where" This was the truth.

"When I leave get that street cleared out there and bring him to the barracks" James said to the officer at the door.

When he got out to the street the first thing he noticed was that Edwards was no longer in the place he had been. James stayed behind the soldiers and raised his hands to quieten the crowd so he could speak. It took a while but in the end there was general quiet.

He stood silent for a moment, what was the best way to say this. He decided on the direct approach.

"The man inside here is not what you are all calling 'The Dolocher'" There was unrest in the crowd as some railed against this news and others groaned in disappointment. James went on. "He did commit the murder of one woman last night but he is a member of a vicious gang and this is his only murder to date"

"How do you know?" someone shouted.

"Because he was in custody during the time of the other murders" James lied. This seemed to placate the crowd a little. There didn't seem any obvious come back to this news and the disappointment deepened in the gathered crowd and they lost the violence that had simmered to that point.

Some of the people looked at the Alderman with sad and disappointed eyes and he felt the shame of not being able to protect them from their fears. They hated him and he was doing nothing to try and change their minds! If only they knew how he yearned to make peace with them all and take away this Dolocher from their lives. He was doing his best to save them but all they saw was Level Low and failure. He wanted to call out to them that there was no 'Dolocher' but he knew this would only rile them up and there would be further trouble.

He went back to his carriage unharried this time. He scanned the crowd one more time for Edwards and the thought suddenly occurred to him that the 'Dolocher' could be among this very gathering. He could have been watching on with glee as someone else was arrested for his crimes. Now he was looking at the faces for what exactly? Was this man going to display evil in his face, in his eyes? He looked at the taller men; Alderman was convinced that it was a large man who was doing the killing, someone who had massive power. He hadn't realised up to now but he still always pictured the murderer to have the build and frame of the blacksmith Mullins when he visualised him and he looked for this man now but with no luck.

As he made his way back to the courts he wondered where Edwards was going to spring from and what information he was going to surprise him with this time. The thought that Edwards was responsible for the crimes had passed his mind many times but he just couldn't make it stick as a suspicion and he didn't know why. It was more likely if he was involved that it was in the capacity as part of a conspiracy to cover up the crimes of another of that menacing 'Hellfire Club' he was part of.

He couldn't get around how powerful these men were and why they would choose to use this power and wealth for such debauchery and so much sinning. They burnt buildings and destroyed property without a moment's hesitation and all in the name of fun and wagers. The dead horse and smashed carriage in Hell came to mind. A night in their company must be more terrifying than a night spent anywhere else in Dublin. They spent most of their time drunk as far as he could see and their money seemed to come from bottomless pits. The grim fact was that if it was indeed one of their number who was this strange and feted 'Dolocher' there was nothing he was going to be able to do about it.

In the end there was no materialization of Edwards that day at all. Just as he was about to retire that evening he heard a knock on the door. He listened at the window and it was a letter being hand delivered for himself. He went out to the landing and called for the servant to bring it to him. He wasn't expecting anything but he felt it must be important to come at this late hour rather than wait until the morning.

It was unsealed and there were no markings on the outside. When he opened it the single page inside read only two words written in writing so neat it would never be able to be attributed to anyone's hand. The letter simply said: This Saturday.

What could this be referring to he wondered. He checked the envelope for more paper and finding none he sought any marks on the paper that give away its origin but again nothing. Though the words were innocuous and harmless they struck a nervous tension through him which he could not explain at first.

It took a few moments for it to dawn on him that the fear he possessed at that moment was that he was holding a letter from 'The Dolocher' himself and that he was saying the he was going to kill again this Saturday! He ran back out to the landing and called out for his servant.

"Who delivered this letter?" he demanded

"It was a young man sir. Not someone I have seen before"

"Did he say who it was from?"

"No sir. He said simply 'Letter for the Alderman' and then he left, ran away"

"Would you know him if you saw him again?"

"I think so yes"

"Tomorrow morning, get someone to cover your duties here and you walk the streets until you find him!" James shouted.

"Sir?" the servant was at a loss as to what to say.

"Check the markets at Temple Bar and then the Liberties, do a circuit there a few times and then come back if you can't find him"

"And if I do find him sir?"

"Bring him to me, by force if you have to" At this the servants face paled a little but he nodded assent and his master went back to his room.

This was not a game he wanted to get involved in. He couldn't think of anything worse than knowing in advance that the Dolocher was going to strike and then not being able to do anything about it. He put on his coat and went out onto the street bringing his servant with him to have a quick look around the local streets for the boy who had delivered the letter. It was a long shot but he had to do something or else he knew he would never sleep tonight.

What of people were to find out about this letter after Saturday and a killing did indeed take place? That would be the riot spark for sure. He did not want to play this game. As he thought of the idea of this being a game he couldn't help but picture Mr Edwards.

Chapter 21

The temperature in the small second floor room on Skippers Lane was pleasant and comforting for the three women who were there tonight. Kate, Mary and Sarah had their hay bags which served as mattresses to them, arranged close to the fire on the wall on the far side of the room from the window. It was a bitter night and they were wrapped in sheets, blankets and had clothes on top of these to aid the warmth of their bodies. They were warmed inside by a vegetable stew Sarah had made earlier with the carcass of a chicken for stock, and weak tea Kate sometimes got from the brothel.

Though she had only taken these two women into her home to get help with paying for it and she intended to have as little as possible to do with them, Kate found that she couldn't help but like them. She was especially fond of Mary, who was making great progress with her injuries. She was going to be scarred for life and sometimes Kate would cry for her when she saw caught sight of one of the marks on her body and she thought about what she had gone through, but she was moving around much better than before and she was getting stronger by the day.

Mary helped at the stalls for small pieces of vegetables which she brought home and shared with the others and she was able to cover some of the potato selling once more. She wasn't able to bring in as much as the other two but Sarah made up for the shortfall so it suited Kate fine.

Sarah was honest and hardworking. She worked at the stalls in the market and she would go about the gangplanks of the ships with armfuls of produce to sell to the sailors who docked each day. They had also come to an arrangement with Kate whereby Sarah would talk about Kate in glowing terms and then would point her out to the sailors as she 'happened by.' This resulted to quite a few on board trysts that might not have happened otherwise and as a result even with Mary's diminished (but growing) earning potential they were living as comfortably as three as most others lived with five or more.

The fire flickered and reflected in their eyes and Kate wondered about what was going on in the brothel that night. It was bitterly cold out and anyone who had to walk the streets this evening was to be pitied. Had it not been for five sailors on a Portuguese vessel at the docks today Kate herself would be out in it. She had to work hard to convince herself that she should not be out anyway, bringing a little more in- even if she went out for an hour, but she managed it and now she was happy and warm and well wrapped up and the dark world outside seemed like a long way away.

"I bet you're glad you're indoors now?" Sarah said when a howling wind whistled through the frames and rattled the glass panes.

"I am" Kate smiled at her. Mary snuggled up a little more in her bed.

"That was a lovely stew Sarah" she said.

"Certainly warmed my belly anyway" Sarah replied.

"Well I think it's time we warmed our throats" Kate laughed and she pulled a bottle of greenish liquid from under her coat and waved it for the others to see.

"What's this?" Sarah said taking it from her hands and peering into the glass bottle.

"Some kind of grog those sailors had today" Kate replied.

Sarah handed it to Mary to look at but she seemed reluctant to take it.

"It's ok Mary, it's only a drink" Kate said "Just have a sip and if you don't like it you don't have to have any more" Mary opened the bottle, the stopper making a funny noise as it came free and she smelled it and recoiled from it.

"Never smell anything you're going to put in your mouth" Sarah laughed

"That's my motto!" Kate said and they all shrieked with laughter as though they were already drunk. Mary lifted the bottle and took a small sip with a look of disgust on her face which all of a sudden brightened into a sunnier disposition.

"It actually tastes alright" she said with a smile. She handed the bottle to Kate who took a longer pull on it.

"I've never had that before whatever it is but it's nice" she agreed. Sarah drank next.

"That feels different to any drink I've ever had too"

They passed the bottle from one to the other and soon they truly were all drunk. They spoke about their pasts and where they had lived before. During the early phase of intoxication they avoided asking Mary anything that might involve her talking about her aunt or worse still of what happened to her but later the conversation naturally drifted to darker things as the bravery of alcohol came over them and they felt they were ready to hear and tell of everything.

"How did your aunt know Olocher?" Kate asked. Sarah looked at her reproachfully but she didn't say anything and Kate knew she was as curious as she to find out. Mary looked into the fire as though she were concentrating on it with great intensity; it felt to Kate that the young girl might be trying to use the dancing flames and white hot embers to distract her eyes from what her memory was trying to show her.

"I never knew that" she replied "One evening he was just coming up the stairs and my aunt had this look of fear on her face that I will never forget" Kate and Sarah looked at one another. "She made me get into the cupboard and told me not to make a sound. She shut the door but it didn't close properly and I could see out through a small gap"

Kate handed the bottle to her but still Mary didn't look away from the fire. She just clasped the bottle and took the longest pull she had tonight before going on.

"He came in and he was angry, he was saying something about her snitching on him and my aunt was saying she had never said anything to anyone. He seemed to calm a little then and he put his hands on the table with his back to her' this was when I got a full clear glimpse of him head on, I was sure that he was able to see me but he didn't indicate that he did" again she paused and the others could see the struggle to go on in her but they waited it out, both so engaged in her story now that they had to hear it to its grisly end. "Then he spun and smashed her across the face and sent her flying. I know I made a noise here as it frightened me so much but my aunt falling made enough of a noise to cover mine. He jumped on top of her then and started hitting her. She was not making any noise but she was trying to defend herself with her hands and arms and then he had blades in his hand and now she was screaming and he was slashing about on top of her like someone having a fit or something like that" there were tears in Mary's eyes now but she looked mesmerised and she seemed unable to stop talking. "I was frozen, I couldn't do anything. Then he stopped and I heard my aunt crying and him trying to get his breath back. She was trying to crawl away from him; I think her senses were probably gone by now, and he let her get a good distance from him. He stood there and didn't make a sound for a while and then he crept up and kneeled down on top of her and whispered something into her ear and that's when he cut her throat"

"Could you hear what he said?" Kate asked.

Mary shook her head but Kate got the sense that she had heard but she was never going to repeat it to anyone ever again. At that moment Kate understood how young this girl actually was; she was fifteen now, fourteen when that terrible thing had happened. She was still a child! And with this thought Kate began to cry as well. Sarah was crying too but Kate hadn't noticed when she had started but she had been a friend of the women so horribly slain that any point of the story would have been an apposite time for her to cry.

When they had stopped and were silent for a while Sarah said to Mary,

"Do you mind if I ask you something about what happened to you?" and Mary nodded, looking at her this time. Sarah looked at Kate as though she didn't know quite how to ask something, looking for support from her but Kate had no idea what she wanted to know and so couldn't help.

"Do you think it was him?" Sarah asked finally and Kate looked intently at Mary to see what she would say.

"I don't know if that's how I felt at the time but that's how it feels now" Mary said and Kate noticed that the young girl was rubbing her arms and then her back where she had been savaged.

"They'll catch him soon" Kate said putting her hand on the child's shoulder. Sarah looked at her in the eyes as though she were trying to see if there was any truth in this.

"Any day now love" she said.

The fire was down to dying embers now and they had huddled their three beds in front of it, their heads feeling the heat and their feet towards the window. The bottle was empty and they were dozing now. None was fully asleep; their bodies for whatever reason fighting the sleep they so needed, their chemical brains looking to keep on going.

When Sarah and Mary fell asleep they seemed to sleep the sleep of the dead. Kate listened to the wind outside as it rattled about and sang through every orifice of all the buildings nearby. The door rattled from time to time as though someone were trying to get in and each time it startled Kate into sitting up and still neither of the other two would budge at all. Each time she would lie back down and wonder why she was not falling asleep; she felt tired but it would just not come.

As she lay there she listened to the breathing of the two women for something to focus on. They were almost in unison but Sarah took slightly shorter breaths than Mary. It was a soothing noise and Kate began to try to get her own breaths in rhythm with the others. She got close but it turned out that she took much longer breaths that them both; while she was awake anyway.

As she listened she slowly became aware of another low noise. It was like another low breathing noise and she wondered if one of the neighbours were breathing heavily in their room? She began to get nervous when it seemed to be getting louder. She looked around the room and told herself that it was the wind and that her mind was playing tricks on her.

There was a movement in Mary's bed and Kate turned to look at her. She was still lying in the same position as before. Then there was another movement and Kate saw it beneath her blankets, she thought it was just Mary's arm or leg but then it seemed too big to be part of this small slip of a girl and Kate sat back in fear, still trying to convince herself that she was being silly, that what she saw was a shadow trick.

When the growling started Kate began to scream and she jumped out of the bed and pinned her back to the wall. She had heard these same growls that night in the 'Nunnery' and they were unmistakable. She was so afraid that she wasn't even trying to get to the door to escape, she was pushing back into the wall in the hope that it would somehow swallow her and take her somewhere safe.

The thing under the blankets grew larger and larger and she could begin to see the outline of something monstrous inside there. Mary and Sarah had not even stirred a little and Kate screamed at them to get up that the monster was in their room but there was no response. She could see the blankets lifting from Mary now as though this creature was wearing them as a cloak as it reared up huge in front of her. Mary's exposed scars were swirling and changing shape and they seemed to grow teeth and they smiled and snapped at her in malevolence. Still she screamed and still no one came to her aid and nor did she rouse her room mates. The cloaked creature began to come before her; much more slowly than she would have imagined it would ever move.

Kate turned and pounded on the wall calling out for help, no reply came, not even someone telling her to shut up, that people were trying to sleep. She turned to face the 'Dolocher' again and she saw that her way to the door was blocked now that she had thought to try to use it. She looked around frantically, half thinking of escape and half of looking for a weapon to defend herself.

Finally she saw what she had to do. She called out once more to try to rouse her fellow women and then just as the creature was upon her she bounded in the small space she had to the window and pushed herself shoulder first through it and plunged to the cobbled street below.

Chapter 22

The children who lived in the lanes and roads off Ushers Quay were always jostling any adult who passed them by with requests for sweets, coins, stories or jokes. They rarely got anything more than a clip round the ear or a curt rebuff but when they did get any of the things they looked for they were over the moon. Though Mullins was the one who lived in their own area they knew they never got anything at all from him unless he had been drinking early in the day and was stumbling home before they had to be home themselves in the evening, but his friend Cleaves was someone they were always happy to see.

He was the type of man who though having none of his own (his wife died in childbirth when they were a year married- the child also passed away) he loved children and was always smiling when he saw them. When he came to call on Mullins the word would go out that he was in the area and when he and Mullins left the house there would be a crowd of children waiting near the door for what he was going to offer. It was rarely sweets or coins but he often had a joke or a story that would have them squealing with delight or disgust - which Is the same as delight in children, and then running to spread his words to anyone who had been unfortunate enough to miss them.

Mullins looked out his window to see Cleaves running into a game of football and tackling the children as they rallied around him laughing and shouting for him to shoot at the goal their team were aiming at. Mullins was impressed with the dexterous movements of his friend and he smiled at the excitement he caused amongst the children. Cleaves was laughing himself as boys grabbed on to his coat trying to get the ball off him and then he planted a shot at goal which missed by miles and he tumbled over onto the ground as he lost his balance taking a few running children with him. He got up laughing and dusted himself down.

"I think that was a goal" he said and the children protested at how far away from the goal it was.

Mullins stepped out of the house and closed his door and turned to face Cleaves who had come over when he saw him come out.

"You ready to tear it up?" Cleaves said smiling.

"I'm aching for a drink at this point" Mullins said.

The children had abandoned their game now and were gathering around Cleaves calling on him to tell them a joke or a story. Their voices were getting rowdier by the second and it seemed even louder with the reverberations off the stone walls. Cleaves winked at Mullins and raised his hands to quieten the children. When they were silent he looked from one to the other with a serious look.

"I only know one story children and it happened in this very place not very long ago at all" he said waving his hand over their heads at the roads and buildings that surrounded them. They were all silent now and their eyes glistened with eagerness to hear this tale. "The most handsome man in the world was walking down through Wormwood and all of a sudden what should he see?"

"A giant?"

"A monster?"

"A pretty lady?" the children called out guessing.

"A football match" Cleaves said seriously "And then he did something wonderful" they were rapt now waiting to hear what he could have done, this handsome man, "he rushed onto the pitch took the ball and scored the greatest goal the world has ever seen!" he cried out and he laughed heartily as the children realised that he was talking about himself and the miss he had just done only moments ago.

"Tell us a real one" they said

"Tell us about the Dolocher" one said and the sound of that name said by a child sent shivers down Mullins' spine. He could only imagine what their young minds must have formed from what they had heard about the killings.

"There is no Dolocher" Cleaves said as though the idea was ridiculous, "Listen I'll tell you one but you have to promise me you won't tell your parents who told you because this one is so scary that you might have nightmares and then wet your beds!" They all laughed and promised that they would not tell and claimed that no story he could tell them would induce them to wet their beds.

"OK, Ok, this is how the story goes" they all crowded in to listen.

"Not many people know this but under Trinity College, deep under the ground there are tunnels and passageways that lead to great crypts and tombs" Already Mullins could see the fear rise in some of the collected eyes "One day there was a funeral and the guard at the gate saw the widow and thought she was the most beautiful woman he had ever seen. Only really important people can be buried there and no one is allowed to visit the tombs once they have been filled. A few days after the funeral the widow came and asked the soldier to let her in to visit her husband's tomb but he told her that he was not allowed to let anyone in. She cried and cried and pleaded and pleaded with him and finally he said that he would let her in just once but that she would never be able to come in again. She agreed and he brought her through the dark and scary tunnels until she came to her husband's tomb.

"A few days later she came again and again she pleaded to be let in but this time the soldier did not budge and he wouldn't let her in. She asked him if he could at least bring a small flower she had in her hair and place it on his tomb for her and that she would then never come to bother him again. The soldier agreed and he went down into the tunnels alone. Just as he closed the crypt door of the woman's husband he heard a scraping noise and he realised with fright that it was one of the old stone doors falling shut. He ran frantically as he knew if the door closed he would be trapped inside forever. Boom! The door closed" The children jumped at the loud 'boom' and then stood looking at Cleaves for a time, waiting.

"Did he get out?" one asked finally tired of waiting.

"No but that is not the scary part" Cleaves went on. "The woman had let the door close because she was angry with the soldier for not letting her see her husband's tomb and she told the soldiers who came looking for him that he had run away with a purse of gold she wanted to put in her husband's tomb.

"A few months later there was another funeral and the day before it a couple of soldiers went into the tunnels to make sure that everything was alright and that the doors were open and room made for the new arrival.

"They carried their fire torches deep inside until they came to a large closed door. This door wasn't supposed to be closed so they knew they had to open it. They used all their strength to open and then on the other side they saw the most gruesome thing they had ever laid eyes on"

"What was it?" they asked

"The skeleton of the soldier who had been locked in standing there with his pike in front of him and all around him there were the skeletons of the rats he had managed to kill before they had swarmed all over him and plucked all the meat from his bones. Some of the skeletons of rats were even stuck on his pike where he had poked right through them.

"Ewwwww" they all said in delight (though some were clearly unnerved by the story) and then Cleaves laughed to set their minds at ease.

"We have to go now so no more stories until the next time" Mullins said and he nudged Cleaves to get him walking before he started to tell them another story.

"Those kids will be up all night" Mullins laughed when they were far enough away from the children.

"One or two maybe but children love that type of thing" Cleaved laughed back.

"What do you suppose they've heard about the Dolocher?" Mullins asked

"As much as you or me, maybe more than you or me"

"Yeah, children can pick up a lot of things that adults miss"

"Adults choose to miss a lot" Cleaves said. Mullins nodded but he wasn't really focused on it.

"You be careful when you're doing your deliveries" he said to Cleaves

"I've been on the lookout since the first killing but I think they happen a lot earlier than when I go out delivering"

"Where do you get all these stories anyway?" Mullins asked after a few more steps.

"A city lives or dies on its myths" Cleaves said tapping the side of his nose and smiling broadly.

Chapter 23

As dark fell that Saturday evening Mr Edwards left the clubhouse on Francis street in ebullient spirits, finishing one last glass of wine in one drain before dashing it against the building directly opposite and laughing as a few women standing nearby were frightened by it and scurried away in terror.

He had received a message from James to meet him at the 'Black Dog' at dusk but he was in no mood for the Alderman's worrying all night and so he sent a boy to tell the Alderman that he would catch up with him later in the evening as he had a few important matters to attend to.

After walking the streets to take in the atmosphere for a while he started to walk towards Temple Bar. He saw the people as he went, rushing from their work to home and those who were alone as he passed looked at him and anyone else who passed them with suspicion and fear. It was this whole fearful atmosphere that had Dublin so electric at the moment and Edwards loved it. He imagined all these people of the lower classes rushing home and making love in case one of them was dead the next day, bottles of alcohol being drunk now in case there is no future to drink them in.

He stopped into a tavern on his way and met a few men he knew from his days in Trinity College and they spoke at length about the state of the parliament and the new taxes being raised. These men would have of course been familiar with the news of the murders that had taken place but they would have no inclination to talk about it as it seemed only to concern the lower classes and those type of people never merited much conversation with people like these. How funny it would be, Edwards thought, if one of them was the victim tonight; that would certainly put the cat amongst the pigeons.

When he left them he went to a gambling house on Crown Alley where he lost what would be a month's wages to a busy trader, in about twenty five minutes. He mingled with the crowd and watched others lose and some win and he had a few drinks while he was there.

After this he left and went to the brothel in the hopes of finding Kate working. He enquired to Melanie but he was disappointed when his favourite girl was not there. When Melanie tried to placate him by saying she would send out someone to find her he replied that he could do that himself and urged that Kate be here more often. He went to bed with Melanie then as he knew she would have to make it up to him to keep his custom. He knew she was well retired but tonight he felt like punishing her for not having what he wanted. That happened at far too many places these days he thought as he left her without paying, feeling the spite of her venomous eyes on the back of his head.

He finally met Alderman James at ten o' clock. The latter was skulking around on Fishamble Street and Edwards came upon him as quietly as he could and then spoke in a loud voice,

"Anything to report so far?" and laughed at James reaction.

"Not yet" James replied looking at him with annoyance.

"How many men?" Edwards asked

"Twenty over the normal patrol"

"Twenty, that's quite a lot!" Edwards exclaimed

"They are not in uniform, I have them on certain streets and I am walking the others"

"Lying in wait as it were?"

"Yes"

"Just like he does?"

"He does not lie in wait Mr Edwards, he follows and then attacks when he sees his chance"

"Or so we think"

"What are you getting at?"

"Nothing, but all we know is that he attacked Mary Sommers from behind"

"Plus the versions of the attacks on the guards at Newgate"

"I suppose" Edwards said and he let his convey that this conversations was becoming tiring to him.

They walked in no fixed pattern the streets and alleys between the Coombe and the Liffey and from Hell to the Four Courts area. From time they would see people coming and going and James would ask them who they were and where they were going. Though most people would lie about what they were doing or where they were going to the Alderman, for fear of what he might say or do to them, none of them seemed suspicious to either James or Edwards.

Midnight came with no event and Edwards regretted not staying in the gambling house and the tavern longer. These streets were now almost deserted and there was none of the fun and the excitement of Temple Bar. He hoped that he was not missing anything good at the clubhouse either. He stopped and looked at James who also stopped.

"I'm very tired Alderman, I think I will retire"

"Fine go, you are no use to me at the moment anyway. Perhaps of you had not spent so much time at your previous errands you might have been better" The Alderman was angry at his drunkenness on a night such as this and Edwards laughed at his simplicity.

"If something happens let me know, but I don't think our man is the type to write letters advertising what he is going to do Alderman. Goodnight" and with that Edwards spun on his feet and walked away chuckling to himself at the stern serious face of the Alderman. How he has let this into his soul he thought as began to walk away in the direction back to the club house.

Chapter 24

The scream had come from close by and James and Edwards looked at one another.

"Circle the block!" the Alderman cried and he ran one way around the building and Edwards the other. As James rounded a second corner he saw something hunched over in the street and he shouted

"You, stop!" and he ran towards it. Whatever it was it didn't look at him but instead set off in the opposite direction.

James bounded after it, glancing at the stricken woman on the ground as he passed. She was alive but badly mauled but he couldn't stop to aid her if he wanted to catch this monster and stop this from happening to anyone else.

"Woman attacked in the lane by coffee house Edwards" he shouted out "I'm chasing the attacker!"

Up ahead he saw the black shape moving between shadows as it kept close to the wall as it ran. Its movements were strange but he didn't get to study them as he chased with the constant changing of the light. It passed by a lantern and for an instant the large back was lit up and he could see that it was covered in dark hair or fur. It was an animal!

It rounded a corner and only then did the Alderman get a sense that it might have looked at him and he saw a quick side profile and saw the massive jaws and teeth for a moment. As he rounded the corner James couldn't see it anymore but he kept on running, knowing now that if he stopped he wouldn't be able to start again. His own clattering footsteps echoed in his ears and then he heard something else from above, he looked up and saw something try to evade his glance on top of the building next to him.

James, without stopping reeled towards the building and jumped up and used the frame of a door to bound himself up towards a window and ledge and then he slipped and held on with his fingers. He got a better grip and he pulled himself up before adjusting on the sill and pulling himself up onto the roof.

When he finally dragged his body up and over the edge he kneeled up and looked around and saw in the distance of a building or two away the creature drop back down to street level and out of sight. James was panting heavily and he couldn't get up from his knees which were bleeding now from the climb up here.

"The Dolocher is on Meath Street!" he called out, desperately hoping that someone on that same street would hear his cry and apprehend the monster. No reply came back and it was quiet save for the Alderman's laboured breaths.

When he got back to where the attack had happened he saw that the woman was on the ground and Edwards had covered her with his coat, all the way up over her face. James looked at him in surprise.

"Literally this minute" Edwards said sadly, "I sent a boy for the doctor but he hasn't arrived yet" James bent down and lifted the coat to look at the woman. Her throat was gashed severely several times but there were not at first glance many more marks on her body. The thought crossed his mind that of all the other victims there had been perhaps they were actually already dead when the worst of their wounds was inflicted- that was if it always went for the throat first, and the idea was on small comfort to him that somehow all the suffering might have been lessened a little.

"You saw it then?" Edwards asked. James nodded. "Man?"

"I couldn't be sure what it was. It was so dark and it kept to the shadows, it seemed to know how to use the light at every turn"

"Did you call out about Meath Street?"

"Yes that was me. He went up on a roof and I couldn't follow fast enough. When I got up there I saw it drop into Meath Street but there was no way I was going to catch up by then"

"Your hands are bleeding Alderman" Edwards said "And your legs, did it injure you?"

"No, I never got near it"

He looked down at his knees and saw the blood coming through the coarse brown wool of his britches and running into his cream stockings. His left knee was still bleeding but the right had stopped and a dark splotch sat around a hole at his knee. He looked at his hands and they were cut badly, he was pumping blood like a bare fist brawler and he could feel his heartbeat in his knuckles as he closed his hand. As he looked at then he noticed he was trembling and he looked at Edwards who was holding out a small bottle for him,

"Just the effect of the chase and the excitement on the system Alderman"

He took the bottle and took a swill and he felt the brandy burn as he did. It was strong stuff. The doctor arrived then and the two men looked at him and shook their heads. He bent to the woman and looked under the cloak.

"Terrible, terrible" was all he said and he stood back up. Both James and Edwards could see that he wanted to ask what had happened and the answer would not be 'The Dolocher' but he was sensible enough not to ask and have himself disappointed.

The soldiers arrived on the scene and James ordered them search the streets in increasing circles from Meath Street but he was not hopeful that they would find anything. The chance to catch the killer had come and gone in moments and James felt that he would never see that dark shadow shifting creature ever again and he would feel the regret of letting Dublin down forever more, especially when the next killing took place.

"I need to get fitter if I'm going to ever be able to catch that thing" he said finally to Edwards when they were alone again.

"Keep this up every night and you will get fitter Alderman" he smiled back.

"I'm growing tired of this cycle Edwards. I walk the street, I have soldiers walk the streets and every time we miss the attack"

"But not tonight"

"The woman is still dead and we don't have him in custody"

"It was close though and next time we will get him"

"I don't want there to be a next time" James said with a terrible sad tiredness. Edwards didn't say anything for a few moments but then he looked at the Alderman seriously.

"If there is no next time we will never catch him"

Chapter 25

The fire crackled and filled the room with brownish peat smoke and the smell of the country. Small bits of wood that had dried in the fireplace were added to the bundle and caused the brighter flames that flickered pleasantly. Mullins looked at it and was lost in the dance. It had been a hard day's work and he was exhausted, too tired even to think about washing. All he wanted to do was sit and be warm and look at the fire until he felt the pull of sleep. This came quicker than expected and he only noticed that he was about to nod off when he heard screaming.

At first he wasn't sure if he was imagining it and then he wondered for another second where it was coming from, was it in the row of buildings or outside in the street. He went to the door and opened it and found he wasn't the only one who had done this, most of the doors held a curious frightened face and they looked to him when he came out.

"Someone's being killed" one of the women across from him shouted at him "Do something!"

Mullins ran in the direction of the screaming but it stopped before he got to the laneway it was coming from. As he rounded the corner into it he saw someone was lying on the ground and as he got closer he saw the blood and the torn clothes that had become so common in this city at night. He leaned down over her and he saw that it was a girl he knew to see who lived on his street, she worked in the tavern on Francis Street. It was a horrible thing to see and like nothing he had ever even imagined before. He had to look away as he took her small soft hand and began to say a prayer for her.

"Get away from her!" a voice snapped at him and Mullins looked up to see three soldiers at the end of the alley. He stood up, blessing himself.

"She's dead" was all he could think of to say.

"Get back away from her, killer!" the same soldier answered.

"Killer?" Mullins said, "I didn't do this!"

"Save it for the magistrate!" the lead soldier said and they approached him with their weapons drawn. Mullins could see that they were careful in approaching him and he assumed it was because of his size and they were afraid he would do to them what they thought he had done to this girl.

"Show your weapon and throw it on the ground!" the soldier barked.

"I don't have a weapon, I didn't do this!"

More soldiers arrived at the other end of the laneway and they too approached with caution. Mullins saw fear in these men too and he looked at his own hands and saw he had his fists clenched as though waiting for a fight. He let them fall flat by his sides and he leaned back against the wall to soften his stance altogether and then they surged forward as though seeing an opportunity and they wrestled him to the ground and shackled him. He didn't fight them; he knew this would make things worse. It was hard though as he felt their rough hands on him and they spared no concern for him as they kicked and beat him as though he were in fact resisting them.

As he was led away he could see the eyes of his neighbours watching him from their doors and windows and the eyes were hostile in this dark and he knew they all thought he had done this horrible deed. He wasn't brought down his own street where the people would have seen him leave after the screaming and could tell the soldiers that he was innocent, that he had been urged by them to try and save the woman.

He wanted to say that the real killer was getting away, had slipped through their fingers while they were blaming him but he knew there was no point. These soldiers didn't care who was innocent or guilty; they brought you to the magistrate and let him decide.

He looked up at the moon and he thought about how close he had come to seeing the Dolocher and he wondered what he might have been able to do if had come across it in the action of killing that poor girl. Would he be able to overpower it or would he simply have been killed like everyone else who had ever seen it; everyone except Mary Sommers anyway.

A man he didn't know caught his eye and he looked at him. He was a gentleman and he nodded at Mullins as he was brought by with an odd half smile on his face. There was something odd about him, something that made Mullins want to look at him some more and when he turned he could see that the man was still looking at him and he met his gaze and didn't let it drop until Mullins was bundled around a corner by the soldiers.

He was halfway down Cook Street, passing his favourite cabin when he realised that they were taking him to the 'Black Dog.' At the gates they knocked loudly and a guard appeared at the hatch and asked what they wanted.

"Open the fuckin door!" the lead soldier ordered.

"Wait here" the guard said and he closed the hatch. For a minute there was nothing and then they could hear the voice of a man who was complaining about something. The hatch opened again and another man peered out at the soldiers and then at Mullins.

"What is it?" he asked

"Open the gate Brick, this is a guest for you for tonight" The gaoler looked at Mullins again.

"You're the blacksmith from just over there" he said "What did you do?"

"Nothing" Mullins said

"Shut up prisoner!" the soldier said and he slapped him across the face.

"Why do you keep dumping people in here, why don't you bring him to the proper prison?" Brick whinged.

"Just open the fuckin gate and stop moanin"

The hatch closed and they could hear Brick muttering something about lazy soldiers and then they heard the locks open and the gate began to creak open to admit them. The soldiers pushed Mullins inside as soon as there was gap enough and four of the six came in with him; the leader telling the other two to patrol the perimeter of the prison, and then the gate was shut.

"Bring us up to the tower" the soldier said and Brick waved at the stairs and nodded for the guard to bring them up.

The steps were hard to take in the way that he was shackled but Mullins could feel how cool and smooth they were under his worn soft soled shoes. When they finally got to the top they pushed him into the room and the soldiers searched him once more as they had when they first subdued him.

"No copycattin your hero" the soldier said but Mullins didn't know what he was talking about and he didn't ask.

The door was clanked shut and locked but two of the soldiers stayed in the cell with him and then two more stood at the bars outside. He thought this was quite odd too but he didn't say anything, trying not to cause any problems for himself. He looked about the cell and it was not as he had imagined at all. It was cleaner for one thing. The floors were flat worn stone and no rats scuttled from corner to corner as damp patches gathered from unknown water sources. The hay on the bunk was not fresh but nor was it rancid and reeking of urine. He heard the soldier telling the guard to send for the Alderman and he went back down the stairs.

Mullins had seen the Alderman before and he felt that he was an honourable man and he would be able to tell his truth to him and have this whole affair cleared up in no time. In the meantime all he was able to do was to rue how slow he had been and wonder if he could have saved that girl if he had not been so tired and falling asleep when the first screams came to his ears. He saw the scars of Mary Sommers and thought about how she had survived this beast.

Chapter 26

It took a long time for the Alderman to come to the prison and when he did Mullins was surprised by what he did. The Alderman came up the stairs and without even looking at Mullins he ordered the prisoner to be released. The soldiers were shocked and couldn't hide it.

"We found him over the body sir!" the lead soldier pleaded.

"Release him" was all the Alderman replied.

The cell door was opened and the lead soldier came in and undid the shackles. As he did he had his back to the Alderman and he made threatening faces to Mullins which he interpreted as 'I'll get you yet Killer.'

"What do you want us to do with him?" the soldier asked when he was done.

"Nothing, you can go back to your patrol. There is a killer loose after all" the Alderman said. "I will take Mr. Mullins down and see him out myself" The soldiers left and went down the stairs.

When they were gone the Alderman motioned for Mullins to follow him and they both descended the stairs and then were let out the gate and on to the square at Corn Market. When they were clear of the square, walking in the direction Mullins had been brought there the Alderman said,

"You have a habit of being in the wrong place at the wrong time"

"Sir?"

"You were questioned about the attack on Mary Sommers weren't you? You walked the streets that night in your leather apron and got all sorts of rumours spinning"

"Yes sir"

"I had some questions asked of your neighbours and was told that you went to aid the woman who was killed this evening. That is why I was so long in coming to the prison. I must apologise for the delay"

"Thank you sir"

"Did you see the killer?"

"No, she was still screaming only seconds before I got to her but when I got to the lane she was already dead sir"

"Have you ever had any suspicions as to who it might be?"

"'Who Sir?" Mullins had noticed that the Alderman had stressed this word and Mullins took it to mean that he held no belief in the Dolocher.

"No Sir, but there is no shortage of savages about" he answered

"True"

They walked in silence for a while until they came to Cook Street. Mullins began to wonder if the Alderman was walking him home to keep him out of trouble. They were across from the whiskey cabin when the Alderman suddenly stopped.

"I suppose you deserve a drink after the night you've had" he said looking at the building. Mullins first thought was how the Alderman knew that he frequented there and then he wondered was he proposing they go for a drink together.

"I think it might be wiser of me to go home and stay there tonight" he said. The Alderman nodded.

"You're probably right. I shouldn't think that anything will happen again tonight but better to be safe than sorry eh?"

"Yes Sir"

They were silent for a moment as the Alderman looked about the street and then he turned back to Mullins.

"I will leave you here, I think I might go for a little walk before I go home for the night"

"Yes sir" Mullins said "Good night Sir" and he walked away leaving the Alderman standing there nodding to himself.

As he walked along Cook Street the urge to have a drink came over Mullins, it was because the Alderman had suggested it. He looked back and he could no longer make out the official on the road anywhere. Would he loop back a little and go to the cabin? Maybe the Alderman went in there and that wouldn't look good him just coming in right after he said he was going home. Should he go to a tavern closer to home? The Alderman knew that he frequented the cabin, would he find out that he had gone somewhere else that evening after leaving him?

He was so full of doubts and second guessing and all the while his legs were carrying him home. He felt eyes on him as he neared his street and he grew angry at the fact that people who knew him all his life and had been neighbours of his could have thought he was capable of killing a woman; it was worse than that- they thought he was the Dolocher. Him, the man who always tried to mind his own business, the man who helped them when brute strength was required to move or lift something! They could all fuck off now, there was no way he was going to do anything for anyone around here again.

He turned right onto his road and made a conscious effort not to look in the direction where the killing had taken place. This made him think about how close it was to his actual home. Although all the killings had taken place in a small area none of them had seemed to impact on his road until now. The Dolocher could have walked up his very road this morning, could have touched his door or his window as it did.

When he got to his door he stopped and looked at the ground and he tried to see the rust that people had thought was blood the night Mary Sommers was attacked. He looked around in the hope of catching one of the neighbours across the road peering out at him but he saw no one.

He sat in front of his now dead fire and took the warmth that emanated from the ashes into his hand for a moment but that only made the rest of him feel cold so he stopped. He climbed into his bed with a piece of bread and lay there peering at the ceiling as he chewed slowly. They think I am the Dolocher. It is not too wild a jump for them to make. They knew he could be violent; having seen him in many a brawl, and he was out at night frequently, in fact he had been out on the nights of all the murders. He just realised this now. Except the one this evening of course he noted as though trying to clear his own name to himself. It wasn't me he thought but it is someone who lives nearby, someone he may see every day walking the streets or working at some merchants. His mind began to flutter between faces he saw all the time, people he knew and people he didn't and he thought that it was no wonder people had thought it was him with all the paranoia and fear that was going about the place.

As he drifted away thinking of who the real Dolocher could be his face rested on the man who had winked at him this evening, the gentleman whose eyes tried to communicate something to him as he was taken to the prison; and in this face he saw something new, something that he was not sure he had seen earlier but that he could see clearly now- that gentleman's face turning up into a sneering smile. The smile of the Dolocher.

He would have to tell the Alderman about this man the first chance he got. A gentleman? Who would have thought such a thing possible and as he thought this he knew that the answer was no one, not even the Alderman could believe that. There would be no point in going to him with this story as it was more likely than not going to end up with Mullins in more trouble and being called a liar to add into the bargain. He would have to keep an eye out for this man himself and see what he could do.

Chapter 27

Alderman James sat in the whisky cabin on Cook Street. He was alone at a table near the back sipping from a tin tumbler, the tables closest to him free as people recognised who he was and didn't want him overhearing what they might be saying. He was quarter way through his jug when Edwards finally arrived.

"I was surprised that you asked to meet me here" Edwards said looking about the room as he removed his cloak, "It's not the kind of place I would associate with you Alderman"

"Sit down and have a drink" James said and Edwards looked at him oddly as he sat.

"You seem odd, gruff even Alderman" he said

"That's the least that these people have to worry about"

"If you have asked me to come here to talk about our mutual friend, I am afraid I have no new information" Edwards smirked.

"Is anything serious to you?" James said angrily "How can you call a vicious killer 'our mutual friend'!"

"No Alderman Nothing in this world is serious to me" there was no smile this time.

James took another drink and he felt the anger course in his blood.

"What is it with your type eh?" he said staring at Edwards who was pouring himself a big drink from the jug. "You meet without a care in the world. You worship the Devil; the very being that will do his best to destroy all mankind and condemn us to eternal fire"

"You make the destruction of mankind sound like a bad thing" Edwards said.

"Don't be flippant tonight Mr. Edwards"

"Something has definitely gotten into you tonight"

"I've had enough of evil, enough to fill me forever"

"What evil do you mean?" James took from his tumbler again and was silent for a moment.

"What does it mean to be decent?" he said finally looking up at his drinking partner.

"It means nothing" Edwards said

"How can you say that. To be decent means you treat people well, you are fair, you do right even when it's easier to do wrong"

"So how many 'decent' people do you suppose there are?" Edwards asked scornfully.

"The point is not how many there are but how many people there are that want to be, or would be if they had the chance. People steal because they have nothing; they fight because they have nothing"

"I know plenty of people who have more than I do who both steal and fight"

"There are exceptions of course but just think if all these people who want to be decent could be decent?"

"You think that everything would be dandy then do you?"

"Why not?"

"Because that is not how people are. People do things because they are bored, because they want what others have, because they want to do them"

"No, I won't believe that. Evil is what makes people do things and evil thrives where there is a lack of decency"

"The evil is there, in the people. That's where the indecency comes from"

"You are not hearing me"

"I think I am but I'm afraid you are wrong"

"I am not wrong. Have you ever seen evil?"

"Only my share"

"No you haven't, but I have. A while after that weaver's riot one of the soldiers whose rifle I lowered tried to kill me. He couldn't live with killing what he considered to be innocent people and it drove him to try to kill me who had made him do it. Do you know what happened to that man?" Edwards shook his head. "I had him hanged"

"And rightly so"

"And that's when I saw evil. It was when I looked in the mirror and I knew that man died because he couldn't live with what he had done, with what I had done. He was right to try to kill me and had I had my wits about me more fully when he tried I should have let him succeed. I killed him to punish him for my crime; that is evil" James said loudly.

"That is human" Edwards said, "You should lower your voice Alderman, I think you are not used to this poison they sell as whisky here"

James knew he was drunk, he knew it as soon as he started to raise his voice. He finished his glass nonetheless and then stood up.

"Come on" he said to Edwards

"Where are we going?"

"We're going to look for 'our mutual friend'"

James felt the cold whoosh through his mouth and into his lungs and he almost stumbled with the increased inebriation this shock caused him. Edwards grabbed him by the arm to steady him but James shrugged him off. He was looking west along the road and Edwards followed his gaze.

"Would you like to go to the scene of this evening's crime?" he asked.

"Maybe" James answered absently "I don't know"

"I doubt there will be any sign of the killer again tonight now that he had satisfied himself"

"I was just thinking about the blacksmith"

"What about him?"

"He has been doing the same thing for years. Going to work, coming to the taverns and cabins and then going home, all the while minding his own business and now because of a killer who has nothing to do with him he has been questioned twice and hauled to the prison"

"Yes I saw him earlier being escorted by your soldiers"

"His neighbours will be suspicious of him now even though he tried to help that poor girl who was killed tonight"

"The people who live around here are ignorant and besides, they have short memories, something else will pique their interest or suspicion soon enough and they will forget all about him"

They were silent for a moment and James still looked in the same direction.

"Was there a letter about tonight?" Edwards asked.

"Letter?" James asked and something was triggering in him as he tried to remember what he knew about a letter.

"The letter from the Dolocher?" Edwards said emphatically.

"Oh, that letter" James mumbled "No, that was no letter from the killer. My man found the boy who delivered it this morning"

"So who wrote it?"

"The boy's mother"

"I don't understand" Edwards said.

"The letter was to warn about a gang fight that took place on Saturday afternoon. The woman didn't want her husband to be hurt as he had been corralled into fighting"

"So she tried to let you know when the fight would be happening?"

"Yes"

"But she underestimated the importance of a gang fight to everyone except herself"

"And I thought it was about the killing"

"Reasonable assumption and he did kill again on the night"

"Pure chance" James said angrily as he remembered the crying woman when he went to visit her home. Her husband had been badly wounded in the fight and wouldn't be able to use his left hand again.

James yawned and stretched his back still looking in the direction where Mullins walked away when he left him earlier.

"I suppose you are right about it being pointless to look for the killer tonight" he said wearily, his bed seeming so inviting now.

"I think so Alderman, best to get to bed and start afresh tomorrow with a clear head"

Chapter 28

The creaking of the ship ropes mingled with the lapping water against the stone walls of the River Liffey. The sailor was on the vessel too long and Kate knew he was probably asleep now having passed out while looking for some more money. It was quite eerie there alone at this time of night at the end of the gangplank and she quickly grew nervous. Images of her absinthe hallucination stalked her mind as she stood alone bringing new fears to the surface along with the natural ones she felt then. She saw the cobbles rise up to meet her face and she shut her eyes against the waking dream. She started to walk away, tired of waiting.

A seagull flapped and scrawked noisily as though disturbed by something up high on the masts of one of the ships as she passed by. Her heart began to pound as she quickened her pace heading for home without another thought crossing her mind.

She cut across the empty market space and the echo of her steps reverberated as though from all around her. She spun wildly looking for someone else- all those same steps could not have been her own. She stopped dead in fear, he mind urging her on but her body refusing to cooperate. Again the seagull flapped and gave out noisily from above, joined this time by an angry partner. She looked up and she saw from where they had flitted, a feather spluttering in the wind not seeming to be falling to the earth at all. She looked at it a moment longer, her fascination overpowering her fear for just that second. It was so white against the black backdrop of clear sky. There was something so terribly beautiful about it and she felt something close to wonderment and a feeling of belonging to the world somehow that she had never felt before. It spun lightly in the sky like a white ovate leaf in water.

The echoes rumbled thunderously around her and the growl was second to them as she spun in shock and caught sight of a black snout and raging eyes before the creature crashed into her sending her sprawling to the ground, sliding away from it a little. The force of the animals attack had sent it too spinning on the wet slippery ground, covered in rotting vegetables and fish dripping. It struggled to get to its feet as Kate did, she caught glimpses of the odd lines of the body of the beast, the jaws opening and separating in a way that looked so unnatural to anything she had ever seen before.

Her glance was momentary however as she got to her feet and tried to pick the least slippery route across the ground they were on. She could hear the slapping of the creature slipping again and she was aware of a small distance between her and her attacker but still she didn't dare look back. She slid a little and she could feel it gaining on her. Her traction was terrible and she felt she was only taking half steps with all the slipping with each footfall.

The idea to scream came belatedly and she bellowed for help as she entered the normally busy alleyway at Temple Lane. In the quiet of the night her screams were like a cannon blast, made all the more loud by the echoing in the cloistered wet streets. She could hear people coming to windows and someone shouted for her to shut up.

A window opened at a building as she passed and she called pleadingly to whoever was up there,

"Please help me. It's the Dolocher!" No one answered and Kate stood there a moment looking around her.

"You should have thought of that before you went walking the streets" someone called from another window higher up in one of the buildings but which one she couldn't make out. She glanced once more at the window she had seen open but she still could see no one there.

She ran now, with a strength and speed she didn't think she possessed. There was anger as well as fear in her run and she cursed the people that would let her die just because of the way she fed herself. A couple of times she glanced behind but she was never sure if the creature was in pursuit or not; she got the impression of dark behind her but there were so many lanes, alleys, arches and doorways she couldn't be sure what it was.

When she could take her burning thighs and lungs no more she stopped and looked quickly behind her before leaning over to pant and try to regain her strength. Her legs felt numb and they were shaking, she wasn't even sure they were going to hold her up for too long. She felt like she was going to vomit and that was when she heard the new footsteps, she was terrified again for a moment but then noticed that they were coming from the wrong direction!

She spun to where to she had been running towards and there was a man coming towards her at pace. She looked back to where the Dolocher had been coming from and she reeled and tried to go in a third direction but now her legs did give out and after one clumsy step she tumbled over her own legs and clattered to the ground painfully.

The footsteps were much faster and heavier now and she turned just in time to see a man whose face she knew but whose name she did not. He was not someone who frequented the brothel but he was definitely known to her.

"What were you running from?" he asked kneeling down to her.

"The Dolocher" she gasped, "I was attacked"

"Where?" he asked already standing up, ready to burst in the direction she indicated,

"Down by the boats, where the market sets up"

"Temple Bar?" She nodded and then he was off and running leaving her where she was.

She sat up and looked after him. He ran towards the creature in the same the way that she had run away from it and she could see that he meant to do violence if he came across it. She watched him into the distance and she listened some more to his footsteps which never let up even after she could no longer see him.

As she looked after him she realised that she was no longer terrified. She stood up and checked the cuts and scrapes on her legs and arms. Her head throbbed and she could feel the blood pumping behind her ears. She looked back to where the man had run and saw nothing. As she looked away she thought she noticed movement and she looked back once more.

She stared into the arch where the carved devil was and she was sure that there was something in the black there, something moving. She began to back away quietly still staring at the black. As she moved she was now sure that there was something there, or someone there.

Her mind wandered to the devil statue, that it might be somehow moving in there but she focused on the black, taking small silent steps towards home as she did. And then she froze.

The silhouette of something not human or any beast that she had ever studied came across the centre of the arch. It was on hind legs but hunched forward, there were no forelimbs that she could see. Those same massive jaws and teeth she had seen earlier glistened almost silver in the light and still the movement of the jaws made no earthly sense; they only occasionally seemed to sit upon one another.

She stood silent as she watched it move again into shadows having passed through the arch heading back down towards Temple Bar. When she thought it was safe to do so she turned on her heels and she sprinted once more, crying and breathing heavily, and she didn't stop until she was home.

Chapter 29

The whisky cabin on Cook Street heaved with people that Thursday evening in early February. Mullins could tell as soon as he came in that something was afoot and he wondered was there going to be a raid on a gaol or an attack on a patrol troop. Everywhere he looked in the place there were wild drunken eyes and rosy cheeks and ruddy noses. Men fell against one another in comradely banter with arms over each other's shoulders; boasts and oaths were flying around the room and there was a low simmering of violence yet undone in the howling atmospheric timbre as every man had some sort of weapon on him.

Cleaves came up to him as he came in and he was as wildly drunk as any of them. His deep blue eyes losing some of their sheen and beauty with the dilation of his pupils.

"You better get some into you boy" he cried to Mullins taking him by the arm and leading him to the bar, "It's going to be a rare night tonight!" he roared this last part and those around him cheered in support.

"What's going on?" Mullins asked; in surveying the room he had seen that Lord Muc and many of his gang were present.

"The Dolocher is going to get a taste of his own medicine tonight!" Cleaves again cried out and again there was more cheering.

"Well make him pay dearly for all the killing he's done!" someone else shouted out and this too was cheered.

"Has he been captured?" Mullins asked. He assumed he had been and that these men gathered were going to take him from custody and do him in themselves. There was no point in sentencing him to hang and run the risk that he could kill himself in the way Thomas Olocher had.

"No, but he will tonight!" Cleaves said almost conspiratorially now, as though the Dolocher was in earshot.

"Does someone know where he is?" Mullins said matching the low tone. He was confused and didn't know what was going on.

"He's everywhere you look" Cleaves said in such a serious way that Mullins almost laughed at him.

"What are you talking about?"

"The pigs"

"The pigs?"

"We're going to kill them all"

As he said this Mullins knew he was telling the truth. Everyone in here bar him and maybe the owner were waiting for later in the night and they were going to sally forth and kill every pig they came across. The myth of the Dolocher and the level of the frustration and fear that his continuing elusiveness created in these people had led them to this desperation; he could feel the belief in these people that if every pig in the city was slain the Dolocher was bound to be among them. There was no point in arguing or trying to change their minds; there had been that much drink had that any naysayer could easily see himself added to the list of victims that night. He didn't want to get involved in this madness but he didn't want to be seen to stand against it. He was after all prime suspect for a lot of people who believed in the human version of the Dolocher. He took the drink offered by Cleaves and he downed it in one before pouring another big one. Cleaves patted him on the arm.

"That's the spirit boy, that's the spirit"

As midnight approached Lord Muc ambled up beside Mullins. The blacksmith looked at him but said nothing, giving a salutary nod instead.

"This is a serious business tonight blacksmith" Muc said looking out over the crowd. Mullins looked too but said nothing. "Violence on this scale is always a serious business" Mullins could feel that he was going to start eulogising about the pleasure of violence again and he took a long drink against it.

"What happens afterwards?" he found himself asking.

"Depends on whether he is killed tonight or not" Muc said "If not the suspicion falls on the likes of me and you again"

"There's no suspicion on me anymore" Mullins lied.

"Maybe not now, but if the Dolocher is not slain by morning you might find that there is a new level of paranoia once the next killing happens"

"You seem sure that there will be a next killing" Mullins said, "What makes you so sure?"

"This thing lives to kill. It doesn't kill for food or in self-defence. It kills with such ferocity that it has to be enjoying it. It's like fucking the top whore in the world to it. It can't go on without doing it"

"Like you and your gang?"

"Something like it" Muc agreed. He seemed to Mullins to be in a state of preparedness (albeit drunk in it as well) for what could be his own death. Mullins imagined Lord Muc envisioning his hand to hand combat with the Dolocher and perhaps himself getting the better of the wild beast (that he believed it to be) and the glory that would come with it.

"The Ormonde Boys will be sorry they missed all the fun tomorrow" Mullins said to change the subject a little

"They are doing their part on the north side tonight" Muc said "This is bigger than what's between us"

At two in the morning they ventured out into the streets. They were led by Lord Muc and they were a frightful sight for anyone who happened to look out onto the street that night. They grouped on the road around him and he gave out orders to spread out in groups of no less than three in all directions from where they stood.

"Remember!" he shouted, like some battlefield commander from Roman times, "Leave none alive. The throat is the best way to kill them! Let this be the last night of killing in Dublin!"

The crowd hurrahed and cheered and then spread out quickly down all side streets and alleys. The first pigs were killed on Cook street itself and by Lord Muc himself, he shoved his pike through their necks and stamped on their heads as he pulled it back out.

These first squeals woke up the night and the bitter cold grew colder still and snow began to fall heavily at almost the first strike against the first pig. Within minutes the ground was covered and visibility was down with the heavy blizzard that whipped up. It seemed to some as though Dublin itself had thrown this haze down to hide what was going on in its streets.

The death squeals of pigs rang out all over the city and the white surface was shocked red by splattering blood everywhere. Pigs lay dead and others still alive though mortally wounded dragged themselves over the bodies or tried to seek out some shelter. Men cried out as they found more of the animals and some men cried out in pain as they either underestimated the strength or the will to live of their enemies. The drunken men wounded themselves and each other with their clumsy handling of weapons their hands were unused to.

The snow continued to fall and the wind grew colder by the minute. By five the last of the known pigs in the city was dead or dying and the last and the most committed of the slaughterers made their way finally home to sleep off their night. What they left behind was hundreds of dead animals; streets and alleyways that were filled with bloodied mushed snow and body parts, weapons lay strewn about where men had given up or been injured. Some of the men had run afoul of soldiers who challenged their behaviour and some were in gaol this morning. A few were holed up in taverns that had reopened to let them in after their work.

When the sun rose at just after eight that morning what Dublin showed the world was what no one expected to wake up to. There was a fairy-tale picture of beautiful snow covered streets and squares; the sun shone and the light the snow threw on the stone walls and the wooden buildings was magnificent to behold. Children came out and rolled snowmen and threw snowballs at one another as their mothers told them to come in from the cold. Footprints were dotted here and there of early risers going to set up stalls at the market or go to work wherever that may be. The city looked amazing and more tranquil than it ever had before.

All this is what was so terrifying about the morning. Less than three hours after the brutal slaughter of upwards of five hundred pigs there remained not a trace of it anywhere to be seen. There were no slayed and open pig carcasses anywhere, no blood lay beneath the new snow that had fallen, there was no longer splashes of viscera and bile and blood on the doors and walls or laneway steps as had been only a few hours before.

Mullins had come home before four but even he had seen enough carnage at that stage to know that something extremely odd had happened over night. He stood at the corner and looked around and it was a different world that before. Mullins could not explain away what had happened and for this reason it was a much scarier world than it had been up to now.

Chapter 30

The cold weather began to set in in early October the following year. The evenings began to lose that light by a few minutes each day and the clouds seemed content to be grey that month with rain falling frequently but for short periods.

Dublin was back to the ways of old and the population had seen a further increase as more came in from the poorer counties in search of work or a means to leave Ireland altogether. Almost every rented room in the city had an additional person living in it compared to the year earlier. There had been massive upheaval in France and there was talk of rebellion in Ireland that added to the excitement. Businesses were doing better than before though there did seem to be more destitute people on the streets than ever.

It was the savage killing of one of these same people that saw the return of 'The Dolocher' after months of silence when the city thought the massive culling of the pigs had gotten rid of it for good.

On a brisk Friday morning a man was found who had been severely savaged by something large. His clothes lay tattered and strewn about the place and his limbs and torso were slashed and ripped repeatedly. There was nothing left of the poor man's face and even his genitals had not been left undisturbed with parts of it lying dismembered a couple of feet from the rest of the body. The place of the killing was a quiet lane well known those who remembered the Thomas Olocher story; Lesser Elbow Lane- the very same place that Olocher's own body had been found half gnawed away by ravenous pigs. The ground and walls were drenched in blood and pieces of the man's brain were coming from the hollow that was his face. It was a truly gruesome sight to behold and one that the woman who first came upon it was unlikely ever to forget.

Alderman James stood at the scene with a sick feeling in his stomach. This was by far the worst thing he had ever seen, worse even than Olocher's pig chewed carcass. He was more tormented however by the thoughts he was having as he looked over the lane for possible clues. Was this the same man whom Dublin had christened 'The Dolocher' or was this a new murderer setting his own cycle in progress? He thought it was more than likely the same man as last year but he wondered where he had been for the last ten months and why he had increased his level of violence for this victim. Had he been somewhere he could not have harmed anyone and this was the deadly result of months of pent up murderous rage? Was it going to begin again just like last year? He didn't know if he had it in him anymore to deal with something like this monster who killed so viciously and was so elusive; the memory came to him of his almost falling from the rooftop that night he failed to catch the beast. The one time he saw it and had gotten close to it. The sting of failure still fresh on his soul.

The soldiers came back to him one by one with news of no witnesses or anyone hearing anything. It was going to be another long, long winter if this was how it was going to have to be endured again. He would have to go to Edwards now and see what he knew and he didn't relish the thought at all, it brought back all the failures of last year and the resulting pig slaughtering madness that had engulfed the city.

He got back in his carriage and had it go down along the Coombe and stop at St Patricks Cathedral where he looked at the impressive building as they slowly passed. He would pray to any God to not have the last year repeat itself. He became lost in thought, as he listened to the slow clipping of the horse's hooves as they went down Patrick Street onto Nicholas Street and into Christ Church, as to the religion that this man could belong to and yet still be able to do such a thing to another human being. Had he no sense of the Hell that awaited him for what he was doing? Perhaps he was pig ignorant and thought hell was going to be full of taverns and brothels like the Hell they were in fact passing through right now. The carved Devil hung over his perception; the dark arch that housed it black and endless in his mind. It felt like the man who was doing this would live there somehow.

When he got home he saw Edward's coach outside and he felt then that he had known that this would be the case. He went into the house and was told Mr. Edwards was waiting in the drawing room. James went to him directly.

"So he's at it again" Edwards said with a smile as they shook hands.

"Possibly"

"Only possibly?"

"It could be someone else"

"Unlikely though?"

"Yes"

Edwards was looking at him with a face that on anyone else James would call concern.

"I can see that this is bothering you but you have to see the opportunity here. If he did not come back you would have no chance of catching him" Edwards was looking at him in animation. James said nothing. "You nearly caught him once and this time around you will catch him"

"I'd rather he was gone forever and no one else had to die" James said.

"That would be terribly boring, Alderman" Edwards retorted with mock contempt, "People die every day in this hellish city but that is all boring; these people are dying with gusto and they are remembered as being victims of 'The Dolocher' as they would never have been remembered by anyone if that were not the case"

"I'm sure they would all rather be alive!" James said.

"Don't be so sure my good man, these people who have been killed weren't living lives like you or I, they were scrounging from day to day, each day harder than the last to feed themselves and their family" Edwards said and he seemed to be in earnest.

James wanted to change the subject. Edwards was enjoying goading him too much.

"What do you make of this latest one?" he asked.

"You see" Edwards said delighted "You are already on board with the notion that this is the same killer as last year" James sighed but didn't object. "This is a ramping up in ferocity which leads me to think that they have not been able to do this for a while"

"I had the same thought"

"I think we should check the prison lists for the last months and see who has just got out and has been in there since the last murder took place"

"Sounds reasonable, I was thinking we should look at the ships manifests as well and see if anyone has left and come back with a few months absence" James said.

"That is good too; you are bound to come up with a few names who will have been legitimately travelling to and fro and the killer if he did leave and come back by ship may have used a different false name on both trips"

"Still worth a look though" James stated

"Indeed!" Edwards enthused. "I have missed this. It was terribly exciting last time"

"Please try not to sound so exuberant about this" James said dryly, looking at Edwards coldly.

"Oh save your looks and admonitions for your criminals" he laughed in return. "I will go to the prisons as I think they will dislike me less than you and I have a few connections there and the money to make a few more" he laughed.

"So I will go to the docks and ask around on the boats that are there now"

"Sounds good, it might not be a bad idea to ask around the market there as well as some of those sellers can be quite vigilant when they want to be. I will go there after the prisons and if you are still there we might meet up"

"Agreed, and if not come to meet me here tonight and we will see where we are"

"Agreed" and with a flourish Edwards turned and headed for the door waving over his head and he did.

When he was left alone James poured himself a large brandy and sat down. His stomach felt ill as he pictured the body from today and he couldn't help but see the body of Thomas Olocher lying beside todays one in that same mucky lane, he could even see that same dog's eyes from before and he couldn't convince himself that the same dog was not there today watching all that was going on and waiting to feast on the meat of the dead. He shuddered at the thought and downed a gulp of brandy before calling for his carriage and making his way to the docks.

Chapter 31

There was another killing only days after the first of the new ones. Another prostitute this time and again the savagery had been more ferocious than any of last year's murders. This woman was so badly mutilated and torn up that no one could tell who she was. She was killed in the alcove where the carved statue of the Devil sat and the whole place was covered in blood and sinews, even 'Old Nick' himself; the cobbled slick with viscera.

"My name is Kate by the way" a voice said from the doorway of the blacksmith's. Mullins turned and saw who it was. He stopped working, stood up straight and looked at her. He was hot and annoyed and tired but he tried his best to be polite.

"What can I do for you?" he asked.

"The Dolocher is back killing again" she said.

"So I hear" he replied.

"People think you are the one going around at night killing" she said

"Some people think that" he replied; the idea of this still sickening to him, to the man he knew he was inside.

"I know it's not true, you don't have that in you" Kate said "And Mary has seen you and told me that it wasn't you. She said she looked into your eyes and they couldn't be further from the eyes of her attacker" Mullins could feel himself blush but he knew his face would already be red from the heat. "I've looked at your eyes too blacksmith and I can see you are a good man"

"Just because I don't go around killing doesn't make me a good man"

"No it doesn't, but something else could"

"And what's that?"

"You must be the biggest and strongest man in Dublin" Kate said as though musing out loud.

"I think there's bigger" he replied. She smiled but this was quickly replaced by a much more serious face.

"The soldiers don't care what happens to anyone around here" she said "they would be happy if we were all dead" He nodded his agreement. "You do care about the people who live here" and again he nodded. "You are the only one strong enough to stop the Dolocher who actually cares about stopping it"

"What?" he wasn't expecting this.

"The killing will just go and on if no one stops it. It seems to be smart enough to stop killing when there are more soldiers around or when groups of men roam the streets looking for it sometimes at night but if you started to look at night, on your own, you might be able to find it and kill it"

"Are you crazy, if I walk around the streets every night and there are more murders I will surely get the blame!"

She looked sad when he said this and this prevented him from saying any more. He waited for her to say something.

"If the Dolocher is not caught soon then it is only a matter of time before me and probably Mary will be dead" she said after a long pause. Mullins knew that there was no way Kate could avoid going out at night if she wanted to be able to survive. "If you do this for me I'll give myself to you" she said meekly. This stunned him and he looked at her again and, though not what was intended, he could only see how beautiful she was.

"What?"

"I could be your wife" she said. "I've seen the way you look at me and it's not just my body you look at" He was sure he was blushing now but he did his best to keep his composure.

"If I ever have a wife" he started slowly and not looking at her now "It will not because she feels she owes me anything"

"We all owe something to the ones we love" was all she said before she left. Her voice had trembled as she was leaving but he couldn't be sure if it was from anger or because she was beginning to cry. Women truly were the most confusing creatures.

147

Chapter 32

On his way to work a couple of days later it was clear to Mullins that there had been another killing, there were so many more people standing around talking in groups than there would otherwise normally be. Though he avoided stopping he knew by the time he got to work that it was a man who had been the victim this time and that the wounds he received were the worst to date, that his face was even missing when he was found.

It was just as he began to open the blacksmith that he began to register and process some of the looks he'd been getting on his way and he felt more eyes on him now. He turned and looked around and it was so obvious that people just looked away as he did. He wanted to ask why but he knew what the answer would be and he couldn't face hearing it at that moment. He opened the door and went inside and waited for his first customer of the day. He busied himself with the work of seeing up, lighting the fires and collecting the tools and he took meticulous care to inspect reach tool as he removed it from the holder in the corner of the room. The heat grew steadily on this cold morning and it was going to be a busy day.

The morning ran longer than usual without a customer and he grew agitated at his idleness. He called the boy in and asked him to go looking for business in Hell and to come back when he had something for the blacksmith to do. As he watched the boy make his way down the road he noticed again that people were purposefully avoiding his line of sight and didn't look at the premises as they passed. He was boiling with anger now and he wanted to shout out to them what they hell they all thought they were looking at but it was the fact that they were not looking that was causing the most hurt. He could feel his shoulders press against his back muscles and he straightened his back and tried to take in some deep breaths.

He longed for the Liberty Boys to bound past on their way to a ruckus so he could follow and take his anger out on a willing human body or any other living thing that might come in his way. He looked out the window once more in the hope of seeing this very thing when he saw Mary Sommers and he stopped dead and stared at her.

He looked at the arch of her back as carried her potatoes and he followed the lines of the scars on her face and hands. He had never looked at her in this way before and couldn't look away now. He saw the white mounds of what looked like folded skin that were her scars and looked at the fear that was evident in even a single step that she took. He felt the warm salt at his eyes and his vision blurred and Mary took on whole other shape in his vision; the shape of a woman unhindered by scars and pain who was going about her business today exactly like everyone else was. Everyone else who was still alive.

But he was not alive anymore.

The anger burst through him now and he turned and picked the table with his tools on it and threw it against the wall. The whole place shook and he stamped on the iron that lay scattered on the floor and he kicked over his stool and the taking up a rod he began smashing the table to nothing until finally, with nothing but small pieces of wooden debris left he collapsed to his knees and his hands dropped to the floor In exhaustion. He cried in this position now and he could see his tears mix with the sawdust and the earth on the floor. Cleaves was gone and not just gone but savagely gone. His cheerful face wiped from his skull and his body torn to shreds; 'the meat plucked from his bones' came to mind and he cried more as he thought about the children's love for him, the man who told them stories but would never speak of the true horror of the Dolocher to them. 'There's no such thing as the Dolocher' he'd told them. There's no such thing as Cleaves now.

He stood up after a while and with a headache he looked at the damage he had done to the place and the image was sobering. He looked outside and saw that people had gathered out there but began to disperse when he looked out.

He went out onto the street and now there were eyes looking at him with sympathy but he ignored this, this was not what he was after. He looked up and down the street for Mary

Sommers and saw her turn the corner up ahead towards Hell. He ran after her and catching up with her called her name. She turned to face him.

"Mary" he said catching his breath again.
"Yes?"
"Can you give Kate a message for me"
"Ok"
"Just tell her I'll do it"
"You'll do it?"
"Yes, she'll know what that means"
"The blacksmith says he will do it, that's the message?"
"That's it, thanks"

"I'll tell her when I see her" and she walked away slowly to continue her work. Mullins watched her for a little and then he began to walk back to the blacksmith.

Chapter 33

Mullins paced his room in agitation and he stoked the fire to keep life in it and get the rush of warmth on his hands, arm, face and chest as he did. Earlier he had received a message from Mary Sommers that Kate would call to his house some time after six when he was finished work. It was just gone seven now and he was tired of waiting, his nervousness getting the best of him over and over again; he didn't know why she was coming. He had said that he was going to try to kill the Dolocher but what did she want to say back to him?

Finally the soft rapping he longed for came on this thick door, so faint that he could have missed had the fire been crackling at all just then. He opened it quickly and the cold whooshed in from outside. She stood there looking at him and it took a moment for him to invite her in. He cursed his own ineptitude with women and there was no wonder he didn't have a wife.

"Sit by the fire and heat yourself" he said pulling a chair from the table to the fireside for her. She thanked him and he nodded. "Do you want a drink?" he asked and then wondered if there was anything he could give her if she said yes.

"Are you having one?"

"No"

"Then I won't, thank you" They were silent a little then and Mullins didn't know what to do with his hands. He pulled a chair in front of himself and rested his hands on the back of it. "I just wanted to come and say thank you in person for what you are doing" she said hurriedly.

"You don't have to do that Miss" he said

"Please call me Kate, Miss sounds terrible on me" she laughed and he could hear nervousness in her laugh that mirrored his own awkwardness at this moment. "You are doing a very brave thing" she said. He blushed and fiddled so much with the chair that he lifted it clear off the floor.

"I'm doing this for revenge" he said as he placed it back quietly on the ground.

"I was very sorry to hear about your friend" she said softly.

"Well, both he and you and Mary Sommers deserve to be avenged" he said and again he blushed, deeper this time.

She stood up as if to leave and he saw that there were tears in her eyes.

"Don't worry" he said "it will all be over soon"

She rushed to him and threw her arms around him and hugged hard,

"Be careful" she said crying now "Don't get yourself killed" He put his arms around her small frame and hugged much more lightly than she.

"I won't" he said. She pulled back and kissed him on the cheek as she did, on the scar that ruined his face and he recoiled a little and let go of her.

"I'm sorry.." she said, not knowing how to go on.

"It's ok, it's just tender in the cold weather" he lied.

She took his hand and looked at his eyes.

"You don't have to do this. I don't' want you to feel you have to"

"I don't feel I have to; I want to do this" Her hand was warm and soft on his and he wanted to squeeze it gently but he didn't dare.

"Don't do anything tonight, I'll come back tomorrow" she said "Will you promise me that?"

"Nothing tonight, I can do that" he said but he had no idea as to why she would want that.

When she left he marvelled at the feel of his face, along the scar where she had put her lips on him. It had been so long since he had felt the sweetness of a kiss and it consumed his evening until he fell asleep that night. He thought he could actually still feel the lingering residue of her on him and he could smell her perfume on his skin. It was the nicest way he had fallen asleep that he could remember in his life.

Chapter 34

Kate went to Mullins' house as promised the next evening. He seemed to her to be slightly less awkward than the previous evening and when she entered he had tea made at the table and the chair she was to sit on was over by the fire and warmed already. She took the tea offered and then he sat down at a chair across from her holding his own cup in his huge hands. It was quite amusing for her to see him like this.

"Did you stay home last night?" she asked.

"Yes" He seemed agitated as though he wanted to say something to her, something that he must feel was important. She didn't say anything to give him an opportunity to say what was on his mind. He was struggling and it was becoming unbearable for her to watch him.

"I think..."

"I don't expect you to owe me anything for doing this!" he said just as she began to talk. She looked at him at a loss for a moment.

"The whole city will owe you our gratitude if you are to kill it"

"I don't need their gratitude, I'm as much at risk at night as everyone else who is outdoors" he said and he leaned forward in his chair to poke at the fire. She felt he did this so as not to look at her at that moment.

"I shouldn't have said that I would give myself to you" she said but he only looked harder at the fire now and she felt his discomfort. "I'm sure you wouldn't want me anyway" and now he did look at her,

"No, don't talk like that, I just meant that you won't owe me anything as it is not your responsibility to get rid of the Dolocher"

"It's not yours either"

"It is now" he said grimly and she felt that he was determined in his own mind that he had to kill this creature now to avenge his friend. She wondered did he think about how if he had tried to kill the Dolocher when she had first asked him would his friend still be alive? If he did it would be a terrible burden on him.

"Every night that I am not at the brothel I see the Alderman out patrolling the streets"

"I've seen him myself"

"Maybe we should go to him and let him know that you will be out at night looking for it; that might make it less likely that you would be a suspect if something did happen"

"Maybe"

"He seems to want to catch it too, when I was attacked he came to my rescue and he ran after it but it got away from him"

"He seems like a nice enough fellow"

"He came and spoke to me after the my attack and he was very nice to me"

They sat watching the fire for a time and he poured her more tea. With the silence between them they could hear some people arguing through the walls next door. Though the words were not clear they could tell it was a couple arguing about something; there was a hurt passion in the tones of voice that murmured to them and joined the crackling fire. A jet of released air from the turf hissed in the grate. Mary looked at him and without saying anything she leaned over and kissed him.

He was hesitant at first but soon he pushed his lips against hers and they met with equal force. He put his arms around her and she felt herself being pulled into his embrace. She sat on his lap and put her own arms around his head and then pulled her head back and looked into his eyes. She saw the fire reflected in them but also something she had never seen before, something trustful and real and yet unnameable; a tenderness for her as a person and not as worker or pastime. She smiled and he looked seriously into her eyes and then he kissed her again and again and they kissed for a long time.

She left later that evening to go to work but neither of them mentioned where she was going. He asked if he could walk her anywhere and she declined.

"I'll keep to the busy streets" she said. As she left she knew that neither of them knew what had just happened between them meant to the other.

Chapter 35

Alderman James' carriage pulled up on Francis Street and he got out and looked at the large house he was about to enter. He knew it well enough from the outside but he had never been inside before and he wondered now what horrors he might find in there. That morning he had received a note from Mr. Edwards to come to the Hellfire Club meeting building at midday. It was just that now and James knocked on the door.

For a while no one answered and then he repeated his knock. Still nothing; he listened at the wood and he heard the sound of footsteps approaching and then the door was unlocked from within by Edwards himself.

"Sorry Alderman but our doormen are under orders only to answer to a secret knock that changes every day"

James stepped inside shaking Edwards hand and waving off his worries about being left outside with the other hand. On first inspection it was not as he had expected. There were no lewd paintings or craven images anywhere to be seen and the sculptures on display were of more Greek inspiration than Satanic. Instead this place was fitted out like the best of the Gentlemen's clubs and taverns in the city. In a strange sense James felt deflated about this, disappointed that it was not the devil's lair he thought it would be.

"You have something to show me?" James said without chit chat.

"I do, follow me Alderman"

They walked up the wide and magnificent stairs. Plush carpets ran up the centre and the wooden steps on either side of this were so polished and well maintained that they could have been stone. The bannisters were wide and smooth and the handrail thick; he imagined the men who frequented here could quite possibly have polished this by sliding down it the whole time (he doubted they had any horses in this place to smash it up.) When they got to the top of the stairs James could hear voices in a room whose door was closed off to the left; there was something boisterous and possibly illegal or immoral going on in there but Edwards took him the opposite direction along a small dark corridor where they came to a panelled wooden door with engravings on it that he couldn't make out in the poor light.

"Prepare yourself Alderman" Edwards said as he opened the door.

In the centre of the room on a huge mahogany table there lay something massive, an animal of some kind covered in black brisling hair. It was enormous and James looked at Edwards who was smiling at his reaction.

"What is it?" James asked though he thought he knew what the other would say.

"Go in and take a look. It's quite dead" James walked in and around the table. Two huge serrated tusks protruded from the jaws of a boar, the largest specimen of which he had ever seen or even heard of. It must have been six feet long and at least three feet high; its powerful shoulder and leg muscles seemed bulging and rock hard.

"The Dolocher?" James asked stupefied. He was so sure that it was a man all this time.

"I think so" Edwards said. No matter what he had heard to the contrary James never thought an animal was responsible, he had seen a human hand in every killing. How had he not seen the possibility of something like this monster being in existence?

"So it was an animal after all" he said, his downcast eyes finding the thick front hoof of one foot and he imagined the power that must have been behind it.

"The tusks are not smooth as you may have noticed and that is what caused the jagged marks on the victims that looked like teeth tearing at them" Edwards said in the vein of a university professor. James felt the tusks and he was surprised at how sharp and hard they were; very much capable of great damage indeed.

"How did it come to be here?" he asked still looking over it.

"One of my 'eyes' brought it to my attention. It was lying dead by the canal bank late last night"

"Who killed it?"

"No idea how it died actually. There are no marks on it that I can see"

"By the canal?"

"Well, the Poddle near the Coombe but only lesser men could call that stream a river"

James walked all the way around the table and looked at the boar from every angle. He couldn't get over the size of it. He had been on boar hunts before, had seen big ones skinned and spread on spits but nothing like this animal.

"What do you intend to do with it?"

"I intend to eat it but I thought you might like to display it for the masses first?"

"This is not what the people want to see..."

"This is what the people want to see Alderman. It is not what you want to see" Edwards interrupted. "This is a bit of a let-down for both of us I'm afraid" he went on.

"I don't see how the ending of a murderous rampage by a wild animal should be disappointing to anyone" James said.

"Let's be truthful here Alderman. You wanted to either catch or slay this beast yourself and get the credit for it with these people and I have to say I had harboured nice fantasies myself of being the one who brought it in- mine was for my own amusement however" Edwards smiled.

"It's over Mr Edwards" James said "That is what really matters"

Edwards nodded ruefully and he looked over the boar himself.

"There is still a way for you to get what you want from this" he said after a pause.

"What do you mean?"

"Well, only a couple of people know this is here right now and they would be discreet if asked"

"I don't' follow"

"Say you and I bring this dirty fellow to one of the back alleys tonight after dark. You cut it up a bit and leave your sword in its throat and then raise the alarm. People will flock to see the hero who has slayed the Dolocher" Edwards was smiling but the smile had an edge to it that James didn't quite understand.

He would be lying to himself if he didn't find this idea enticing, at least at that moment it was mentioned but he couldn't do something like that.

"No, thank you for your concern but it is I that I need to appease not the people of this city"

"So how would you like to announce this?" Edwards asked.

"Perhaps we should bring it to Corn Market and show it there. That is after all where everyone assumes is the start point to all this, why not end it there as well?"

"Why not indeed. I'll get it down there in a covered cart for say 3 o'clock?"

"Yes that sounds fine"

"Please though Alderman, try to keep the people under control. I am really looking forward to getting stuck into this at dinner tonight" and this time Edwards smile was broad and malevolent and James could almost sense an anger that this beast had died not at Edwards hand or that it was no longer going to be around to entertain him.

At the appointed hour the cart pulled up outside Newgate Prison and the Alderman stood up on the back of it and called out to the crowd to gather round. There had already been something of a gathering as news spread that the military presence had grown since midday around the prison. Now more came out from shops and other businesses and formed a half moon around the cart at the gates of the 'Black Dog.'

"I have some great news for Dublin today" the Alderman began and at once there were ripples of talk in the crowd. "The Dolocher is no more!" he said and he pulled the white sheet covering from the boar with a flourish and stood back as the collected gasp of the crowd came at him.

They rushed forward to the edge of the cart pushing the cordon of soldiers back against it and rocking it violently enough that James almost lost his balance. There was no menace in the crowd and the soldiers understood this and they gently jostled them back by a foot or two.

"Be orderly, you will all get to see" James called out as he got better footing in the cart.

"Who killed it?" someone called out

"We don't know, it was found dead on the banks of the Poddle" James said. Slowly as the people looked with wonder on this porcine phenomenon a sense of relief and celebration began to sweep through the crowd. The most doubtful of them looked at this savage animal with its huge bulk and vicious tusks and it all fit. The rumours were of a huge black pig- this was a huge black pig. Boars were known to everyone to be dangerous at the best of times and the crowd began cheering with laughter as though it were some festival they were at.

"Good riddance!" "Hooray for the death of the Dolocher!" "Hooray for the Alderman!" "Hooray for the dirty water in the Poddle!" the crowd was calling out many things and they all laughed at this last one.

As James enjoyed the festivities he became aware of the crowd parting and gathering again around a girl who was making her way to towards the cart. The people she passed fell silent and they watched her as she limped towards the beast. As she got closer James saw that this was Mary Sommers, a girl who had been badly attacked by the monster and still showed the scars of her ordeal.

"Let her through" he said to the soldiers in front of the cart.

He watched as she came trembling up to the side of the cart and she looked along the flank of the animal.

"Would you like to come up here to see it?" he asked and she nodded yes. "Lift her there" he ordered and a soldier on either side of her took her by an arm each a lifted her easily onto the bed of the cart. She looked afraid but James beckoned her to come to his side of the cart and see the creature better. She was trembling as she did, all the while staring at the serrated tusks.

"Don't worry Miss, he is quite dead I can assure you"

She stepped to his side and she looked down at the boar seeming to satisfy herself that it was dead. Then she bent down and to the Alderman's shock she began to feel the tusks and even more bizarrely she lifted the lifeless eyelid of the creature and looked at the glassy eye beneath. She stood back up and then whispered to the Alderman,

"This is not the Dolocher"

James could feel the blood drain from his face.

"What do you mean?" he asked of her trying not to let the crowd hear what he had said.

"Those are not the eyes I saw when I was attacked and those are not the teeth that tore me up" she said almost in tears now.

"There, there dear" James said taking her into his arms and then whispering "Don't say a word to these people, please. I will talk to you later" Mary looked at him and nodded and then made to move away, "Let her down men" he called to the soldiers who lifter her down. "I will come to your house in one hour" he said quietly to her as she was lifted away from him.

Mary dropped back into the crowd and went back through the people the way she had come. He could see the men and women she passed look at her with pity and some patted her on the back as she went by but then the crowd was swelling and the tide was being pushed forwards towards the cart and he lost sight of her. He didn't think she had said anything to any of the people she passed on the way and for this he was thankful.

The cart rocked with the force of the people craning to get a better view and James got down to the ground and began to extricate himself from the fray. He couldn't suppress it but there was a strange sense of glad in him that this creature was not the Dolocher and that it was indeed a man he was looking for. There was a still a chance for him to been seen differently in the eyes of the populace.

As he climbed into his carriage he looked out over the people as was his habit and looked for those eyes. The eyes that Mary Murray had seen.

Chapter 36

Kate was trying to get work at the docks when she heard a ripple through the crowd at the market. There was some news spreading fast through the stalls and here and there cheers went up and a lot of people began to leave the area through the alleys at Temple Bar. Kate rushed to the vegetable stall to see what was happening.

"They've caught the Dolocher!" the seller said and she seemed like she was itching to leave her stall and go and see for herself.

"Really this time?" Kate asked hoping for a yes.

"Seems so, a man who was up there said there is a giant boar up there at the 'Black Dog' that has massive tusks like saws and it way bigger than any normal pig he's ever seen"

Without saying anything else Kate walked as fast as she could towards the prison to see for herself. She was trembling as she neared Cornmarket and she could see the large crowd from a long way off; some were cheering and there was a general sense of relief that was palpable in the air. As she got to the back of the crowd she could hear people talking of the size of the beast and how vicious it looked.

As she tried to push into the crowd, many of whom were leaving having seen the monster and become tired with being crushed in the crowd, she noticed Mary emerging from the group. She looked pale and in shock and Kate called out to her but Mary made no indication that she heard her and she kept on walking in the direction of where they lived.

Kate was torn as to whether to go after her or to go and look at the boar. She called out one last time to Mary and then she felt herself push into the crowd as she made her way towards the gate of the prison. She couldn't see where she was going as everyone around her was so much taller than she and she bumped against peoples backs and ducked under outstretched arms until finally and without warning she stumbled into a tiny clearing and fell against the side of a wooden cart and found herself face to face with the monster.

She screamed in fright and pulled back from it as people turned to see what had happened. A hush fell over the crowd as clarification on why someone had screamed in that way was forthcoming. Kate ignored the eyes on her and she looked back at the face of the boar lying on the cart. It was huge and muscular and dark as she had expected. She looked at the long tusks and she was afraid again as she thought of what they could have done to her that night had the ground at the market not been so slippy. She began to cry and her hands were shaking uncontrollably and she felt some friendly hands on her back lead her away from the sight of the killing creature and towards the back of the crowd and out where she could breathe again properly.

When she was feeling better she thanked the two women who had taken her out and she began to make her way home where she assumed that Mary had gone, she wanted to make sure that she was alright because after all Mary had had a much worse encounter with the Dolocher than she'd had and was probably in a bad state right now even though the thing was lying dead on the cart for all to see.

When she got in Mary was at home sitting in front of a small fire that she had just gotten going and there was a look of terrible sadness in her eyes.

"You saw it?" Kate asked

"I saw the boar, yes" Mary said softly.

"Are you feeling ok?"

"Did you see it?" Mary asked her back without answering.

"Yes, it was horrible"

"It wasn't the Dolocher" Mary said.

"What?" Kate couldn't understand why Mary would say this.

"I got up beside it and I opened its eyes and they are not the eyes that I saw the night I was attacked"

"But it has to be Mary, they eyes might be different when the thing dies"

"Did you see it when it attacked you?"

"Yes but only glimpses as I was doing my best to get away and was afraid to look back at it"

"Did it look like that thing they are parading around out there?"

Kate thought for a moment but she had found for a long time that what she could remember of the night she was attacked often became confused with the hallucinations she'd had the night they drank the Absinthe in the room and now as images came to her of the attack this new shape and size of the boar was what she thought she remembered.

"I don't know, it's very confusing" Kate finally admitted.

"You saw the eyes though as well didn't you?" Kate though for a moment and then on this point she was sure.

"Yes, I definitely saw the eyes" Mary nodded and looked back at the fire.

"If you go back up and look at the eyes on that boar you will see that it not what attacked you in the same way that I did"

Kate sat down and put her arms around Mary and squeezed her against herself.

"Well it was a nice few minutes believing it was dead" she said smiling.

"I'm sorry" Mary said

"It's not your fault"

Outside they could hear people going about the streets telling those who hadn't heard yet and the descriptions of the monster wafted up and in through the thin walls of the building. They were all going to be very disappointed, and for the second time, that the Dolocher was not what was captured. Kate looked at Mary and she felt pride at how brave this young girl was, and she squeezed her again, only a little tighter this time.

Chapter 37

People scuttled along the streets and disappeared down laneways and through doors in fear. Mullins stayed in his shop knowing full well what was happening outside. He worked on with the white hot metal, dousing it in water and laying it on his anvil to be hammered. He waited for the doorway to be darkened as he knew it would and when it did he turned to face Lord Muc.

The gang leader had a mean look on his face and his eyes were wide open and yet somehow calm. Outside there were about twenty men with various arms and improvised weapons with wild excitement in their eyes and their bodies jittering from the effort of standing still. Mullins didn't bother to let him speak,

"I've no interest"

"I'm not here to ask you to fight"

"I'm not fixing any weapons either"

"I'm here to ask you to just come and watch today"

"Why?"

"To see what you are missing"

"I'm not missing anythIng"

"You don't think you are anyway" Muc smiled.

"So you think I will go and watch you lot fight and I will be so impressed that I will want to join up?" Mullins sneered but Muc wasn't fazed by this at all.

"I don't think you will be impressed but you will be stirred and that's all I'm looking for" Mullins thought for a moment what to say next.

"If I go an watch and am not interested at all will that be the end of your pestering of me?"

"That sounds fair" Muc said.

"Where will it be?"

"At the Poddle, where the Dolocher was found"

"When?"

"About half an hour"

"Right, I'll follow up in a few minutes" Muc nodded and he went outside and headed in the direction of the mentioned river.

Half an hour later Mullins was up on the site where the fight was going to take place. He took up a position on a high wall that would allow him to watch and at the same time would not permit him to become involved too easily; he had no intention of joining in but one of the Ormonde Boys might mistake him for one of the enemy and attack him if he was at ground level with the rest of them.

The Liberty Boys were congregated around Lord Muc who seemed to be performing some kind of ritual. He was saying something over and over and his eyes were closed as he put his face up to the sky. Mullins could not make out what he was saying but he had a feeling it was something in Irish. Then Muc got down on his haunches and was still saying something but this time the gang were responding and as Lord Muc began to rise from the ground they became ecstatic and began hooting and hollering until finally Muc was standing bolt upright and he held two weapons into the air and the others went wild in praise of it. Mullins looked closely to make out the weapons he was holding, it was like two short swords but as though made of bone and with sharp serrated edges. He looked closer still as they were held up against the sky and he knew then what they were. It was the tusks of the Dolocher!

At that moment a gang of about forty young men appeared from the west -the Ormonde Boys must have done a wide westward arc to avoid detection by the troops as they crossed the river to come to this fight. They arrayed themselves in front of the well outnumbered Liberty Boys and stood shouting obscenities.

Without hesitation Lord Muc let out a feral howl and charged at the enemy, his gang in close proximity behind. It seemed to take the other gang by surprise and they to a man stepped back a little. Lord Muc met them at full charge and slashed savagely with the tusks of the Dolocher and two of the enemies fell immediately. Mullins was stunned as he saw the rest of the smaller gang pummel into the shocked lines of the

Ormonde Boys. All manner of weapons were swinging and poking and slashing and thrusting and screams and grunts of pain and effort rang out all over.

The congealed grouping began to break off into smaller man on man fights and the circumference of violence expanded dramatically with some men even splashing about at each other in the river itself. Mullins had heard of these gang fights before but he had never actually seen one. He was amazed by how willing to maim and slice their enemies these people were.

There was eye gouging and hammers smashing into cheekbones, knives were cutting into flesh at every part of the body and fists and kicks were supporting the weapons wherever they could. Mullins was drawn to the vision of Lord Muc in the middle of the melee. He looked so powerful and seemed oblivious to any of the wounds that were peppering him as he doled out more serious damage to his foes. He slashed and hacked at them with abandon and pretty soon the Ormonde Boys were running away (those who could were anyway) and Lord Muc called a halt to proceedings.

Everyone stood up and looked about; both Liberty and Ormonde Boys, and saw the damage that had been done.

"We have the day" Lord Muc said "Take your lads back across the Liffey" he said to a few enemies who were still there and possibly able to do anything for their mauled allies. There were men on the ground in extreme pain and some who were clearly dead. The whole thing had lasted only a few minutes but the damage done was immense. Lord Muc held up the tusks and his men cheered. He looked at Mullins with a smile as blood ran from his forehead and neck and he breathed heavily to oxygenate his muscles.

Mullins sat on his wall with his arms crossed but he smiled back and gave the gang leader a nod of appreciation before looking at the fallen men once more; their bodies still and their clothes rustling slightly in the breeze. He couldn't lie to himself. He was intrigued by it all and he had found himself so involved in the fight in mind that he felt almost as though he had been down on the ground in the thick of it.

Chapter 38

Mullins wrapped up warm as he was ready to go out for tonight's hunt. He had eaten heavily after work today and he slept as much as he was able to after this. It was now eleven O'clock and he was ready to start pounding the streets. He was nervous but also hopeful. There was every chance he felt that he could come across this killer and be able to take him down and deliver him or it or whatever the hell it was to the Alderman. He had heard (and seen) that the Alderman often patrolled the streets at night doing this very task and he hoped to run into him early tonight to let him know that Mullins would also be doing the same from now on. He took up a leather pouch in which he had concealed a knife and went out the door into the dark cold of Dublin's night.

Kate had come to him at the smithy yesterday to let him know that both she and Mary were in agreement that the boar that was being trumpeted as the Dolocher was not what had attacked either of them and that the real killer was still loose and would kill again as soon as it could. Mullins couldn't say that he was entirely disappointed with this news as he had felt a pang of regret when he heard about the boar that he had not been able to avenge Cleaves and Kate and Mary; but now his chance to do damage to this killer was back and he was fully prepared to do it. His body still buzzed with the energy of the violence he had seen at the Poddle a couple of days ago.

Kate had taken his hand in the smithy and again said that he didn't have to do it, that she was afraid for him now but he clenched her hand and told her he would be fine and as he did he thought about taking her from the life she had once this was all over and he did his best to communicate this to her in the touch of his fingers and the look in his eyes and he felt then that she had understood; and that they both understood that for their future to have a chance of ever existing, the Dolocher would have to be gone.

It was a cold hard night and he could see his breath vapour in front of him as he walked, the light behind it making it look like the smoke from a pipe. He walked briskly to try to keep warm and he had no set plan as to where he was going to walk. He knew the general area he was going to stay within but he decided to let his whim and instinct guide him at every junction he came to. As he came to corners or crossroads he would look in all directions and if he saw breath rising but no person to breath it he went that way; if he saw a person walking alone he went that way, if there was something just too eerily silent about a street he went that way.

He was at this for about half an hour when he saw someone he recognised but who he couldn't place for a moment. He followed the man at a distance and he observed his walk and his mannerisms as he went along seemingly without a care in the world. It was not the Alderman but someone else he had seen recently; the man who looked at him so oddly when he was taken to the 'Black Dog,' that's who it was! The gentleman he suspected as a possible killer, how could he not have recognised him immediately.

Up ahead the gentleman turned a corner onto Francis Street and was out of sight so Mullins quickened his pace and rushed around the corner in the hope he was still in sight only to find the point of a sword almost prick into his throat, he stopped dead to cease the impact being caused by his own weight.

"You should be more careful about skulking about the streets at night blacksmith" the man was smiling at him

"Put your sword down" Mullins growled

"Not until you take your hand from the blade in your pocket" the man said nodding to where Mullins was indeed unfurling the leather pouch. He stopped and pulled his empty hand into sight.

"My name is Edwards" the man said lowering his own weapon.

"Mullins"

"I know who you are and what you have been accused of by your own neighbours and I can tell you sneaking up on people in the dead of night will not enhance your reputation in the slightest"

"I'm out to make sure that my name is cleared once and for all"

"How is that?"

"I'm going to catch the Dolocher and kill it"

At this Edwards burst out laughing and this perplexed Mullins.

"How are you going to find him? The Alderman has been out all night many times and has not been able to find him yet"

"I think I may have found him" Mullins said angrily

"You think I am the Dolocher?" Edwards asked still amused.

"I don't see why not, I've seen you around the streets at night and you are pretty handy with that sword"

"I haven't been questioned by the law about any of the killings which is more than I can say for you my good man" still that smile on his face.

"The Alderman knows I've had nothing to do with the murders"

"Does he know you are out at night now looking to get yourself killed?"

"He doesn't know but if I see him I will tell him"

"I can assure you that I am not the Dolocher and that if you are going to be wandering the streets at night you and I may see a lot of each other"

"So long as I don't see you killing anyone I'll not bother you again" Mullins said with a sarcastic sneer but again Edwards only laughed.

"You are lucky you are talking to me, any other gentleman would have you in the stocks for talking to them like this" Mullins didn't know what to say to this. "Carry on blacksmith and the best of luck to you. If I see the Dolocher I'll tell him you're looking for him" and he laughed heartily once more as he turned and walked away.

Chapter 39

The next killing followed not long after the boar was displayed to all at Cornmarket just as Alderman James had feared. He had known by the face of Mary Sommers that they did not have their killer. He went to her that afternoon at her home and both she and another victim told him that the boar was not the Dolocher. As he made his way to the site of the murder James was already aware of who the victim was; it was the gaoler at Newgate Prison James Brick and it was the one person who could have been killed who could reignite the nonsense of revenge from beyond the grave by Thomas Olocher.

The body was as badly mutilated as the delivery man Cleaves' had been, limbs and stomach torn to shreds and the face all but smashed into the skull, brains and skull spattered around the ground about the head. Edwards as always was standing nearby but James wanted to talk to the soldiers first for their version of events, if there was any. There wasn't much to go on apparently; the guards at the gaol said that Brick left without saying anything at about midnight as he did sometimes and they saw no more of him after that. The body was found in a tiny alley at Cutpurse in front of some businesses that were closed for the night and so yet again there were no witnesses to the attack, some people a street to either side had heard a short sharp scream but nothing after that.

James then went over to Edwards to see what he had to say.

"The gaoler" James said

"The perfect person to keep the rumours alive" Edwards replied. As he said this James suddenly thought that Mary Sommers would have suited this role as well and he called a soldier over and ordered him to go and patrol the street where she lived until daybreak and to report anything he thought was suspicious. Edwards listened and then said,

"You think she will be targeted again?"

"I do now. There is something that feels staged about this, something almost theatrical and the perfect way to go from here would be to kill Mary Sommers"

"A definite human mind behind what you propose" Edwards said

"I have felt so all along but I let what I saw that night I chased him cloud my judgment"

"What motive could there be behind all this killing? Some of the people were linked to Thomas Olocher but the rest have seemed almost random"

"That's what is so hard to say. I have searched high and low for any relatives or friends of Olocher that might have had reason to feel they were avenging him but I have come up with nothing. He seemed to have no friends and no family"

"My own searches have come to the same conclusion"

"So why would anyone want to carry on in his name?"

"Maybe they aren't but people are just reading into it that way?"

"No, I think if he wanted to be known for what he was doing he would have changed his killing method once the rumours of the Dolocher started to spread"

"On another note and to confuse things further there is something I think you should know about" How could things get any more confused James thought,

"What?"

"The blacksmith, Mullins, has been out wandering the streets at all hours the last few nights and he is not going to taverns but just walking all the streets where the killings have taken place"

"Why is he doing that? Him of all people"

"He says he is going to catch the Dolocher" Edwards smiled

"He'll get himself killed or worse still people will be convinced now that he is the killer and he will be killed by a mob"

"He has his own theory as to who the killer is" Edwards grin grew even wider now

"Who?" James asked, eyebrows arched.

"Me"

"Why does he think that?"

"He has seen me out on the streets at night and I get the impression that he doesn't like the look of me one bit"

James's own doubts about Edwards resurfaced here and he thought again about how he knew more than he let on. It was possible that he was indeed the killer, he was always out in the middle of the night and he had plenty of places he could hide after he killed but then hadn't he been with James when one of the murders was committed, Again it came down to the idea that Edwards was an accomplice at best and if that was the truth there was no way that the Dolocher was ever going to be revealed and brought to justice unless James or Mullins or a victim was able to catch him and overpower him.

"Well, this paranoia will get the better of most people" James said "There are some who probably think I am the killer for the same reason" and as he said this he wondered if it might not be true; and why not him Alderman Level Low, he's killed before hasn't he? Multiple weavers and who knows how many else? He realised for the first time, and as he did he was dumbfounded by his own naiveté, that if he didn't catch this killer he was going to be associated with it; the Alderman who walked the streets at night, who was always around when the murders were committed. Was there no end to the bloodlust of this man? How could he have been so silly as to not to have been able to see how guilty he could look in the eyes of the very people he was trying to redeem himself with. The idea of rumours, the same thoughts he had about Edwards, now came to him. If the Alderman is not the Dolocher he knows who is and he is protecting him. He saw the faces of the men in the whisky cabin on Cook street who left the free tables around him and didn't want him in their company- he'd thought it was because he was a man of the law but it was because they were afraid of him and what he might do to them if he came across them at night on their way home, or what whoever he was protecting would do to them. If the law was the murderer who was ever going to be able to do anything about it?

"This Brick fellow used to sneak out to meet a woman" Edwards said and James snapped back to the moment.

"Sorry?"

"Brick leaves the prison a few nights a week to see a woman, the tale goes that she is paying off her husband's debts in another way to keep him out of prison"

"Who is this woman?"

"I'm not sure of the name yet but she lives in Wormwood and that is probably where he was going tonight"

"That would make sense I suppose"

"You don't seem interested in this information?"

"I'm not really, if he does this a few times a week he could have been observed many times by the killer and easily targeted"

"You don't think the husband might be a suspect?" James looked at Edwards

"For all the crimes or just this one?" he asked

"That's what I was wondering now myself. We find the name of the woman and that leads us to the man and then we can see who he is and what he is about"

"Worth a try I suppose" The Alderman was still thinking of his own guilt and his own stupidity.

Chapter 40

Mullins could feel the many eyes on him as he approached the shed he was told Lord Muc was in. The atmosphere of distrust and fear was palpable and men fidgeted as they pretended to focus on the tasks they were doing. Mullins got to the doorless frame and knocked on the wood but did not go in.

"What is it?" a harsh voice called out.

"It's the blacksmith" Mullins called in "I want to talk"

"Come in"

Mullins stepped inside to what looked like a makeshift workshop. Some of what he saw he recognised as poor variations on his own work tools and equipment and the rudiments of any other numbers of trades. There were animal skins and fabrics spread about in one corner; weapons and farming tools in another. Piles of scrap steel and wood lay strewn about the floor, leaving almost walkways between them like those in a well-trod field or forest. Lord Muc had his back to Mullins and he was hammering on something. Mullins stopped about ten paces from him and waited.

"What is it you want?" Lord Muc asked when he stopped banging, he lifted a metal looking ball on the end of a club; it seemed to Mullins that he had been just knocking some sharper points into the metal to be used as a mace of sorts.

"I want you to help me catch the Dolocher" Lord Muc turned at this and a broad smile spread over his face.

"We already tried that, I lost a few good fighters that night and with fuck all to show for it in the end" he said as though the memory was funny to him.

"I'm not asking for another rampage, just some of your people to help me patrol some nights"

"And what's in that for me?"

"Anyone of your men could be killed as things stand on any night and you yourself have been harassed by the soldiers thinking you are the killer"

"My men can look after themselves and as long as you are around I'll never be the chief suspect for the killings"

"So you won't help me?"

"I didn't say that"

"Then what are you saying?"

"Join us and you'll get all the help you need" Lord Muc looked at him steely eyed and seriously. Mullins stopped a moment; he had partly expected this but hoped it wouldn't come to it.

"Help me for a week and I'll join you in one of your fights"

"Not good enough"

"Five nights?"

"I'll give you three this week if you fight with us next Saturday morning"

"Fair enough" Mullins said and he knew he had gotten less than he would have liked from the bargain.

"If I help you win well, I get a week of help afterwards" he demanded

"You'll get help based on how you perform"

Chapter 41

Kate was in the brothel on Friday night when Mr. Edwards came in and beckoned her over. She looked to Melanie who nodded for her to leave her current customer and go to Edwards. When she got over to him he said,

"You're coming with me to my house"

"I'll have to ask Mel..."

"No time for that, just come on" he said and he pulled her by the arm out of the brothel and out to the street and into his carriage. There was something different about him tonight Kate thought but it was that drunken moodiness he sometimes had. She wanted to ask him what was wrong but she was afraid of his getting angry.

"I hear you have been seeing a lot of the blacksmith" he said after a few minutes silence. She looked at him but he was looking out the opposite window.

"A little" she said knowing from the past that there was little point in lying to this man who seemed to know everything that was going on in the city no matter how trivial.

"I need you stay away from him from now on"

"What? Why?"

"I just need you to do it"

"Not without a reason" she said, she was angry that he thought he could control her life outside of his use of her as a prostitute.

"It's for your own safety"

"I'm perfectly safe with him, damned more than I ever am with you" she said and now he did look at her.

"You think you are safe with the Dolocher?" he said and there was no sneering smile that made what he said all the more scary. Mullins was the Dolocher? He had the build and the strength? But... No! Why was she letting him make her think like this. She knew who he was, what he was.

"What are you talking about, he is the most gentle creature there is"

"That's what's so suspicious, when he is working and sober he is as meek as a mouse but when he gets a few drinks in him or his anger is up he is vicious and loses control at the drop of a hat"

"I know he has fights in the taverns sometimes but what man doesn't do that?"

"Listen Kitty, I have thought him innocent along the way but I have my doubts now and I can't shake the idea that you are in danger around him"

At this her heart jumped and she grew nervous. Did Edwards have feelings for her? It was more than she was capable of not to think of herself living in the warmth and opulence of his home. And at once she felt she was betraying Mullins for whom feelings had grown organically over time and much to her own surprise. Her heart was pounding as she didn't hear what he said next but she knew he was saying something, she looked at him, saw his mouth move and his eyes as he looked on her- was there anything in those eyes? There was but what it was would have been impossible to detect and decipher.

"What did you say?" she asked

"I said I will get you into the brothel full time so you won't have to walk the streets anymore"

"I don't want to be in the brothel seven nights a week!" she said and this was the first she knew of it and the first that she found that she must have assumed that Mullins was going to take her as his wife someday and that she wouldn't have to work as she did now; would not be able to work as she did now, and that the brothel was now something that caused a send in her stomach that was pure revulsion.

He was looking at her now with an odd look as though she were mad or had said something totally unexpected.

"You are happy to walk the same streets where people are being killed all the time?"

"No" she said but didn't know where to go from there.

"I see" Edwards said and now he did smile, that sarcastic smile he had that tinged on evil and made him so unpredictable.

"What do you see?" she asked insulted.

"You think he will marry you" He was right and though she said no with her face she knew he knew he was right. "You think anyone would marry a prostitute?" the sneer thickened momentarily and then fell into a piteous face.

"Plenty have before" she retorted lamely.

"If this blacksmith is as good man as you claim then why on earth would he marry a hooker?"

"I think you better let me out here" she said not looking at him, she was furious and more so because part of her knew that he could be right, probably *was* right. She knew what was intimated between Mullins and herself but it was something that had gone unsaid, something that didn't necessarily have to come to pass, a future unwritten. He could decide that he couldn't marry a street walker despite how she knew he felt right now; he was clouded by the first woman of his life and Kate knew that love or the illusion of it can be thicker than any winter fog, and could lift just as quickly.

"I'm not finished with you yet" he said

"I don't care, I want to get out"

"If you leave this carriage you will never work in that brothel ever again, or any brothel for that matter!" he snapped at her.

In that instant she saw a light open up and the beams of chance came shining through. If she was put out of the brothels would that not be the first step to being something else, someone else? She would have no choice but to do something else as she couldn't live with what she made on the streets alone. She could see herself telling Mullins that she was quitting the life she led; he didn't have to know she was being forced out of it or that she was doing it in the hope of a better life with him. Should she get out or stay and degrade herself with this wild and dangerous man to keep sure of food on her table? The light was too strong,

"Let me out please"

Edwards looked at her with what she read as disappointment before tapping the roof of the carriage and shouting for the driver to stop and let the lady out (he called her lady.) When she stepped down to the ground he caught her arm and she turned to look at him.

"Be careful, nobody knows who the Dolocher is" and there seemed to be genuine concern in his face and his voice- he was so hard to understand.

"I will be Mr. Edwards" she said quietly and she stood there a moment as the carriage pulled away into the night towards the Liffey to cross over to that house where she had fleeting fantasies of living, where she would have been warm and safe tonight. She looked around and wondered what to do and then she walked briskly along the most populated routes back to the brothel.

Chapter 42

Saturday morning. Mullins had been in bed only three hours when he was back up for a new day. Without pausing to rethink his plan he had whisky first thing on an empty stomach. He was going to get drunk this morning and use this as his way to get through the fight he had agreed to with the Liberty Boys.

As he drank he thought about his futile run of nights where no sign had been spotted of the Dolocher anywhere. He let Cleaves drift into memory and he focused on the day that he heard about his murder, remembering the nods and looks in his direction as he had made his way to work and how he knew the gory details before he knew who it had been who was taken that night. He could hear a couple of children outside arguing about something trivial and he thought of the love the children had for Cleaves and the time he game to them with jokes and stories. This was starting to make him melancholy so he tried to focus on the murder again and he saw images of blood stained laneways and then he saw Kate being attacked down by the boats and how lucky she was to escape and this made him really angry; Mary Sommers bent and scarred body made itself visible now and again the anger grew. He stood up and took hold of one of the large heavy chairs in his room and he squeezed it, feeling the thickness and how satisfying it would be to smash it to pieces against the wall or even throw it through the window. He resisted this urge; he'd thought himself a lesson about the cost of such things when he thrashed his shop a while back.

He stormed out of the house and headed for Lord Muc's place with red descending all around him and he had no idea of the weather or people around him. He pushed through crowded choke points where sellers were gathered and he pushed past the first layer of Lord Muc's men who were taken by surprise.

"Come on let's go!" Mullins shouted from outside the workshop where he had met Lord Muc the previous week.

Lord Muc appeared in the doorway and smiled at him.
"You're keen"

"Let's go now and get this over with"

"We can't go now, there'll be no one there if we do"

"Can you not arrange it earlier then?"

"That's not the way we do things blacksmith. It's only an hour away so you won't have to wait long"

Mullins was losing the worst of his fury now and he felt a little tired and lightheaded.

"Come in here and have some sausages" Lord Muc said and that sounded just about right to Mullins then. He went inside and the shed was warm with cooking and body heat. The smell of frying sausages was intoxicating and he was handed a plate with three thick ones on it.

"That'll be enough to see you through the battle today" Lord Muc said as he bit a large chunk from one of his own. Mullins bit into one and some fat splashed out and burned his lip. The men laughed and Mullins gave them looks that silenced them all except their leader. "You've been drinking I see" Lord Muc said giving him a once over.

"So?"

"Nothing wrong with it I suppose, some men do that but I find it dulls my senses and I don't enjoy what I am doing as much during the battle"

"Well I don't plan to enjoy myself"

"You feel that way now but I promise you it will be a different story when I ask you after it all"

"I doubt it" Mullins said and to change the subject "How long will this go on today do you think?" Lord Muc thought for a moment and then said,

"They were humiliated the last time and it was over in a flash so they will be looking for both revenge and to save face so I imagine they will be fiercer than usual today and it will go on a bit. We won't surrender and they are on home turf so they can't surrender so it could be all out today" His men were nodding at this, some looking into the frying fire and seeming to realise that today's battle was going to be a different one. "This could be a very sad day blacksmith, you may be involved in the last battle between the Liberty Boys and the Ormonde Boys, if they lose badly enough today it could be the end of them" Lord Muc looked sad at the thought.

With half an hour to go Lord Muc began to rally his men with mentions of the last battles and the wounds those still with them had received and invoking the names of the dead and crippled. Mullins had been given a top up on his drinks and he found himself getting into the group frenzy as they filed out and onto the street to head to the north side of the River Liffey where they would fight their enemies for perhaps the last time.

When they arrived at the site where the fight was to take place the enemy was already there and they were a sight to behold. They had taken a leaf from Lord Muc's book and invoked the Dolocher themselves, they were covered in strange garments and wore crudely made pig head dresses as they taunted the Liberty Boys.

In Mullins' current state of mind this was a taunt too far, he was exhausted from prowling the streets at night looking for this beast and he was drunk now and emotional and even though the Ormonde boys would have no of way of knowing the he was single handedly trying to catch the Dolocher every night for all of their benefit he was furious at their insult to him. He looked at Lord Muc and seeing that he was not ready to get going yet Mullins made the decision to fly at them on his own.

"Bastards!" he shouted as he ran at them, towards the dead centre of them where the leader most likely was. As he ran he was vaguely aware of Lord Muc shouting something at him but Mullins was focused ahead and he could see the look of shocked fear in the faces of those he was about to engage. They had never seen him before and in full drunken, enraged flight the blacksmith was a sight to behold. He crashed into the front row of men with no weapon in his hands and sent many of them tumbling to the ground with his force. He felt searing heat at his shoulder and across his chest and he knew that one or two of them had managed to cut him with their weapons as they tried to defend themselves.

Mullins fell to the ground with his own velocity and took another two down with him as he punched hard into their faces. He could hear the stampede of feet as the Liberty Boys joined the fight behind him. The two men he fell with were unconscious and Mullins sat up and looked about him. There were weapons flashing in the light everywhere and the tearing of flesh and costume was all around. Lord Muc slashed his huge boar tusks across the face and chest of a man who fell at his feet in agony and then he was standing over Mullins.

"You should have waited for my go ahead blacksmith!" he said angrily as he lashed out at someone else who had approached him. Mullins didn't say anything, stood up and finding a discarded club he began to swing it around his head and bring it down on any of the people around him who were wearing the pig costumes. Men were falling all around him and the carnage was unbelievable, Mullins found himself stepping over people as he hunted down the last of the dolochers who were doing their best to avoid him while trying to fight off their Liberty boy's opposite numbers.

Soon and with bated breath Mullins had to stop swinging the heavy club and as he dropped it to the ground he noticed for the first time the blood and pulp on it that was god knows what part of the men he had waylaid with it. He looked around and saw some of the costumed men run away, very few though as the rest of them were either crawling around on the ground in agony or else they were lying still and possibly dead.

Lord Muc was beside him now again and they looked around the scene together.

"You looked like you enjoyed that blacksmith, there was barely anything left for the rest of us today" Mullins looked at him and he felt disgusted with himself.

"I didn't enjoy one second of that and I won't ever be doing it again" he said.

"There mightn't be a chance to do it again, that may very well be the end of the Ormonde Boys today. A good few of those on the ground there will never be able to fight again" Lord Muc said nodding the crumpled bodies in the mud.

"I'm going home" Mullins said trying not focus on what he had just done.

"Be careful on the way, the troops will have wind of this by now and you could be stopped anywhere on the way back"

"I don't care" Mullins said and he walked away back towards the river.

As he walked he could feel now that his hands were shaking and he was feeling ill in his stomach and felt like he was going to vomit. He kept seeing the eyes of the men, those terrified eyes, behind the Dolocher masks and he heard again the cracking and crunching of bones as he smashed into one after the other. What had he done, were any of those men dead?

He couldn't think properly and he had senses that he had caught the Dolocher, had in fact killed it and this whole ordeal was over. He thought of Kate and he knew that the Dolocher being gone had something to do with her but what? He was tired and the cold was starting to come in on him. He had no idea what he had just done or what he was going to do. He walked.

Chapter 43

Kate knocked lightly on Mullins' door and waited for an answer. She could feel the eyes of neighbours and local children on her back as she waited for an answer. None came so she knocked a little louder this time in case he was in bed. She really needed to see him right now or else she knew she would lose her nerve. There was still no answer and she tried looking in through the window but it was impossible to see inside as a thick brown blanket hung over the window to keep in the heat.

Just as she was about to walk away she saw him turn the corner from Ushers Quay and come into his own road. She smiled when she saw him but it dropped quickly when she saw his demeanour and then she saw the blood on him. She ran the short distance to him and he didn't see her coming and was taken by surprise when she grabbed him asking what had happened to him. She wondered had he been out all night, had he been attacked by the Dolocher, was it dead? He pushed her gently away as he winced in pain and said nothing but continued on to his house. She followed him and when he went in she followed there too without waiting to be invited.

"What happened to you?" she asked again but louder

"I was in a fight" he said

"With who?"

"The Ormonde boys"

"A gang fight!"

"Yes" he took off his shirt and there were a few slash wounds that still oozed blood on his back and side. She grabbed a bowl of cold water and a cloth and began to wipe at him

"What the hell were you doing in a gang fight?" she said and her anger made her rub the more roughly.

"Ow" he said and he stopped her hand and took the cloth from her "I can do that" She let go of the cloth and stood back a little.

"Why were you fighting with them?" she asked again

"They're helping me at night looking for the Dolocher"

"And this is the price you have to pay for it? To nearly get yourself killed and make yourself useless to anyone?" she could hear the tears in her voice before she felt them in her eyes.

He looked at her on hearing her upset and he had the confused look of an animal on his face. He didn't understand why she was so upset.

"If you go looking for the Dolocher with wounds all over yourself and tired from fighting he will kill you for sure" she cried.

"I'll be ok" he said and he dabbed at another of his cuts, this time on his arm.

"You won't be ok!" she said "I know I asked you to do this but now I am asking you to stop, please"

"I can't stop until it's done" he shouted back at her and there was an immediate silence in the room. He looked away first and went back to his wounds.

"If you keep on doing it you're not doing it for me anymore" she said

"It's only now that I am truly doing it for you Kate" he said in a serious voice and he looked at her. "Before I was doing it for revenge, out of anger but now I'm doing it because I want you to be safe, I need you to be safe" he said. She stepped forward and took his hands.

"You can make me safe without killing yourself" she said now crying more than ever. He took her into an embrace and pulled her against him and she could feel the hotness of the naked strong torso against her and right now she did feel safe.

"If I don't kill it I can never be sure you'll be safe" and this was said with the voice of someone who was final in their own mind, who had made the irrevocable decision that would guide their life from then on.

"What will we do when it's gone?" she asked submitting to his will, knowing that she could do nothing in the face of that fog that she was now enveloped in as well.

"Anything you want"

"I don't know what I want"

"Does it involve me?" he asked and she could feel his body tense up for a rejection that he thought might come.

"That's the only thing I do know for sure" she said and she felt that strong embrace once more and she squeezed back as hard as she could.

Chapter 44

Four loud knocks on the door. This was how Alderman James always announced himself at premises. He was wary of knocking the tree times that felt natural to him because of its connotation with death and his own connection to death in the minds of the people. He looked to Edwards who was with him.

"What do you suppose she will tell us?" James asked while they awaited the door.

"Lies" Edwards replied smiling brightly

"And what of the husband?"

"Who knows at this stage Alderman; all the people who seemed likely culprits have turned up clean in all searches and questioning so it stands to reason that it is someone we haven't come across yet"

"There are an awful lot of people we haven't come across yet" James said as the door opened.

A plump woman with a red face, from being over a large pot most likely, peered out through the smallest crack in the door. When she saw that it was two gentlemen she opened it wider and stood to almost military attention.

"Evening sirs, what can I do for you?" she asked, her voice trembling with the fear of the upper classes.

"Is Mrs. Caldwell in?" James asked politely.

"Yes sir I'll get her for you"

"Is Mr. Caldwell home as well?" Edwards asked as she was about to go.

"I'm not sure sir, I can check if you like"

"No, that's ok, Mrs. Caldwell will be fine" and she went back inside to get her.

Only a few moments later a good looking woman who James was sure was once a beautiful woman came to the door and stood before them timidly.

"Mrs. Caldwell?" James asked and she nodded. "We want to ask you about the murder of the man who was killed at the laneway at Cutpurse the other night"

She looked to them both in fright.

"Me?" she asked, teetering on hysteria.

"Yes you" Edwards said harshly "We know you didn't do it but we also know you and he had a little arrangement"

"He had an arrangement and I just had to go along with it" she said almost in tears now.

"Calm down now dear" Alderman said "We just need to know was he on his way to see you the night he was killed?"

"I don't know, he just came when it suited him. I think he had people who told him when my husband was out in the taverns or the gambling dens"

"Do you think you husband could have killed him?" Edwards asked bluntly and she was clearly taken aback and already James knew they were on to yet another loser.

"No, have you not seen my husband? He has been crippled by his drinking and late nights, he couldn't even kill me if he tried" she said.

James indicated with a nod that he thought they should go, that they were wasting their time.

"Well at least you won't have to pay his debts with your body anymore eh?" Edwards said tipping his hat and walking away before she had a chance to respond. She looked to James and he too tipped his hat.

"Sorry to have disturbed you madam but we have to follow up on everything" and he left her standing at the door dumbstruck after her ordeal.

"Why did you talk to her like that?" he asked Edwards when he caught up with him.

"Like what?"

"Like she was the scum of the earth"

"Oh, I don't know, isn't she?" James didn't quite know how to answer this. He felt sorry for her at the door but before that and now since they left he could feel his natural revulsion at what she was doing, had been doing, rise up again.

"I'm growing weary of this Alderman" Edwards said stopping at a street corner.

"What?"

"This whole thing. It has been going on too long, there has not been enough drama to it"

"Drama!"

"Yes, finding bodies in the morning is one thing but where are the eyewitnesses to tell the tales and for us to see the fear in their eyes as they do, the survivors who are so rattled that they can't even talk to us without jumping at every shadow?"

"I've told you before not to talk like this" James said. Edwards didn't reply but he had the look of a bored child looking around the streets.

"I have the Dolocher!"

The cry came from streets away and for a moment James was not sure that he had actually heard it. Edwards was running and then James was beside him and they saw others coming out of houses and looking out first floor windows. People were looking around and asking where the call had come from and soon James and Edwards were in a group of people looking in all directions waiting for another call.

"Over here!" someone shouted and the crowd ran to a thin laneway not big enough to hold them. Edwards and James could not get through the throng and they could see nothing though the focal point was clearly just up ahead.

"Let me through!" James cried but there was no budge in the crowd.

Could it be? He wondered, was the Dolocher just up ahead lying there? Was it dead, alive, dying? What was it? Who was it? It was killing him but his authority was holding no sway with the blinded people here and he had to push and push and push until he finally got to the opening.

Chapter 45

Mullins went to the door of the tavern and looked outside.

"It's coming down like horse's piss out there" he laughed "have you got a cloak I can borrow?"

"There's a large ladies one someone left here but that's all?" the barman offered also laughing.

"It'll have to do" Mullins said and he took it from him and threw it over his shoulders and pulled up the hood. "Must have been a fine sized woman who owned this?" he laughed when he was able to pull the hood up and close the cloak a little at the neck.

"Never saw her" the barman said "Thank God!" and they both burst out laughing.

"Thanks" Mullins said as he stepped outside.

"Look after yourself"

When he was out in the rain it didn't seem so bad, the cloak was actually quite thick and he could get a faint smell of perfume inside its hood. He wondered what type of a woman who smelled so good would be in a tavern to leave a cloak like it behind her.

Something crashed to the ground not far away and took his attention. It had been a woman emptying a bucket out the window and onto the street a little from him. She was on the second floor and he gave her a theatrical bow as she closed the window. He looked back at the streets around him he saw the street sign for Braithwaite Street and it triggered a memory he'd had. He was on Pimlico road and just beyond him was the entrance to Greater Elbow Lane which in turn housed Lesser Elbow Lane, the place where Thomas Olocher's eaten body was found.

With the courage and curiosity of drink in him he walked resolutely to this site and he stood looking at the thin lane and trying to imagine what the soldiers had seen when they found him. There was another noise behind him but he didn't turn this time thinking it the woman emptying buckets again on Pimlico.

He grew tired of standing here and he made his way towards Meath Street. It was quiet as he walked down that echoing street and the rain was down to a light shower. He passed Cale Alley and Engine Alley and then Earl Street onto Meaths Row. He thought he heard something like a dog growling but he couldn't see any dog around.

As he passed the narrow entrance to Hanbury Lane something black and full of gleaming teeth launched at him from the darkness. It was powerful and with his inebriated state Mullins lost his balance and fell to the ground. The creature came up on top of him but Mullins had his strength still and he grabbed hold of it and pulled it towards him to stop any slashing motion of those wild teeth, to take away the opportunity for motion. As he held the struggling animal it felt strange, the muscles not reflecting the size of the frame. He lashed out a few times at it he felt that it was trying to get out of his grip, returning blows with hooves that seemed to be on its chin and upper lip. The blows came as though from punches from a man and this didn't make sense at all in Mullins' frenzied mind. He lashed out with his knee at where he thought the groin might be and the creature doubled up and lashed somehow with the centre of his back at his face and he felt his nose break and his eyes watered as he let go of the monster.

It scrambled up from him and Mullins, though not seeing, swung his legs and tripped the animal as it tried to get away. It crashed down and Mullins grappled on the ground with it as his sight came back a little. He pounded blows into the abdomen of the creature and its skin and fur seemed to shift and soften his blows as though the creature was hollow in places. The teeth came at him and it was then that Mullins knew he had seen this motion before. He had seen it when Lord Muc fought with the tusks as the Poddle that day. This was a man he was fighting, a man inside a costume with his arms inside a serrated gauntlet and the part of the back that had struck out at him was in fact the head covered by the fake animal skin.

With this new theory in mind Mullins began to rain down blows through the 'jaws' and into the hard lump between them. His blows got harder and harder and he threw his head in there for good measure, the blades of the teeth catching him from time to time as he did and slowly the creature began to lose strength and finally lay moaning the moan of a wounded man.

Mullins sat back against the wall exhausted and called out loudly.

"I have the Dolocher!" He could hear doors opening and running feet slap against the ground and people asking one another where the call had come from.

It wasn't long before a crowd had gathered in the rain to see the spectacle of the blacksmith and the Dolocher both lying wounded on the ground, the creature moaning like a man and blood spread over both.

Mullins pulled himself up against the wall of the building behind him and got into a sitting position. As he did he saw that the man in front of him was trying to get to his knees to crawl away. Panic spread in the people gathered,

"It's getting up!" someone shouted.

"Relax people, he's not going anywhere and he swung his large fist down on the back of the creature where he estimated the man's head to be and it slumped again to the sodden ground. "It's a man in costume" Mullins said as he tried to catch his breath, his eyes still streaming and his nose bloody and painful. The people huddled a little closer and soon they were jabbering in agreement,

"It is a man!" "Looks like boar skins all sewn together" "Let's see who it is" a soldier who had arrived said.

"Leave him until Alderman James gets here" Mullins said. "Has he been sent for?" The soldier stopped and looked at him and then stood thinking for a second before issuing an order for the Alderman to be sent for.

As he lay there bleeding Mullins was growing weak and sleepy. He could still hear the people all around as they chatted excitedly about the end of the Dolocher. Their numbers had swelled dramatically by now and every window and door frame held as many faces as they could. He was entering that strange consciousness of near sleep when he heard Kate saying something to him but when he opened his eyes she was not there. He closed them again and she was thanking him and she was wearing something cream that he had never seen her in before. He knew she was safe now and he nodded at her thanks. He was warm now and everything he heard sounded strange and echoed in his head.

Finally he felt a pair of hands on his shoulders shaking him and he thought it was the Dolocher having awoken again but when he tried to raise his arms in defence he found they only went half way up before he felt a terrible pain and he had to put them down again. He opened his eyes and he saw the smiling eyes of Alderman James.

"You did it!" he was saying over and over.

Mullins sat forward again and began to get a clearer picture as to what was going on around him.

"Who is he?" he asked the Alderman.

"Let's find out" he replied with a smile and he nodded to the soldier who was there already..

They both watched with great interest as the soldier took his knife and finding a hollow space he sliced into the front of the costume and then pulled it apart. As the hide skin ripped and pulled apart Mullins looked on with interest in his head he figured he was going to see Lord Muc or else Edwards and this was what he was hoping but as the top of the head was revealed he saw that it was not going to be him. This man was quite bald on top, a thin sheen that almost reminded him , with his hat off of course, of.....

And then he saw the bloodied face and it was him! Without his cap on and Mullins pushed back against the wall in the horror and shock and he looked to the Alderman who glanced back at him in wonderment. There in front of Mullins being disrobed as the Dolocher was none other than Cleaves! The friend he had thought was so savagely killed that nothing was left of his face and not much of his body; the man who was so beloved by the children of the Liberties and who told ghost stories and was always ready for a laugh, who Mullins had sworn an oath to avenge! He was the Dolocher! He was alive! He was the one who tried to kill Mary Sommers and his beloved Kate and now tonight had even tried to kill him, a man he had called many times over their lives his best and only true friend.

"Cleaves!" he finally managed to say and he saw the head bobble on the body of the half costumed Dolocher and he saw those placid peaceful and beautiful eyes gaze upon him and there was such sadness in them.

"I didn't know it was you Tim" he croaked and all Mullins could say at that moment was,

"I know"

"And she wasn't your lady friend at the time either"

"I know" Mullins was still in a daze, his nose aching and his mind unsure as to what was happening.

"Who is this man?" the Alderman asked looking at Mullins

"This is Cleaves who everyone thought had been one of the victims of the Dolocher"

"Cleaves! Then who is the man who was killed?" the Alderman shouted at Cleaves

"He was a man from the country who was unlucky enough to have the same build as me and be out on the streets with nowhere to stay that night" Cleaves said after he rubbed blood from his mouth.

"Why, Cleaves?" Mullins asked, still in a state of disbelief, he wanted to hear that he'd had no choice somehow that there was some coercion behind that he could not fight back against but he knew in his heart that this was not going to be what he was told.

"For Dublin" was all Cleaves said in reply to this.

"What the hell does that mean?" the Alderman shouted at him but Cleaves didn't answer and his sorrowful eyes were again on Mullins as though he were willing him to understand what he was saying.

And Mullins did understand what he was saying but not then and not for a long time afterwards when Cleaves was hanged, when the rebellion of 1798 failed and the parliament was dissolved and Dublin was ruled directly from London. In his own twisted way Cleaves believed that a city, a people even, lived on only though the stories that were left behind when they were gone. Cleaves could see the writing on the wall for Ireland, knew that it was only a matter of time before it was no more than a province of England and he wanted true Dublin to survive this.

He donned the mask of the Dolocher, his arms covered on the flanks with serrated steel shards that many thought were the teeth and jaws of the beast, and he killed and terrorised in the middle of the night in the name of history, the preservation of history. He wanted to invoke a Dublin that could never be forgotten by those who would live there for ever to come, a Dublin that was of Dublin and not of London. For that reason he made as sure he could that it was never an English person he killed and he never attacked anyone from the army, he didn't want the Dolocher to ever be associated with freedom fighting or nationalism. It had to be a myth that grew and grew and changed as the years went by into something intrinsic to the city, something that could never be separated from its narrative.

And that stands to this day. The Dolocher is still known in Dublin over two hundred years later but if you ask anyone today who Cleaves was they will look at you with a blank expression and tell you that they do not know.

A city lives and dies by its myths.
The End

Thanks for reading. I hope that you enjoyed this book. Please leave a review at your local Amazon site or you can contact me at www.europeanpdouglas.com with any comments you might like to make.

About the Author

European P. Douglas was born in Dublin, Ireland in 1978. He always had an interest in writing but only began to take it seriously in his early thirties. As of September 2014 he has close to 2,000 readers and he is happy to hear feedback from any of them.

He is married to Aisling and together they have a son called Harrison and another baby due in Jan/Feb 2015. They also have a cat called Paris and a new Fish in currently being discussed.

Printed in Great Britain
by Amazon.co.uk, Ltd.,
Marston Gate.